Second Impressions

By Rand Gilbert

Chapter 1: A Surprise

Lacy Jennings stepped off the 4 train and into a cacophony of city sounds that felt entirely foreign. She had grown up surrounded by the hum of cicadas. Coral Springs wasn't much for traffic – the morning school bus came to pick her up during the school year, and her dad's old clunker drove down to the record store he somehow still kept open, even now—probably mostly due to tourists and the support of a close-knit community. But back in Coral Springs—a place Lacy always thought was oddly named, being in the middle of Colorado—traffic just wasn't much of a problem. Even in college, she'd had a relatively quiet experience, attending a community college just a half hour's drive from home, so she could be close to family.

But now, it was time for Lacy to find her way in a new world. And that new world was filled with noise. Cars honked impatiently, people shouted into their phones, and the air buzzed with an energy that made her both excited and nervous. The smells of the city were different, too; a hot dog cart. Someone smoking. Days-old garbage that hadn't been picked up. It was a far cry from the scent of grass and morning dew.

She adjusted the strap of her bag on her shoulder as she looked up at the towering buildings above. This was her new world, and despite some hesitance, she was determined to make it work. Failure was not an option; she would not return to work at her dad's store, even if it meant living in a closet-sized apartment and lugging her laundry six blocks in the dead of winter... the city was her new home.

The job at Carver & Co. had been a stroke of luck—an entry-level assistant position at one of the most reputable advertising firms focused on the automotive sector. It wasn't exactly where she'd imagined herself after getting a degree in marketing (she admittedly had hoped to work at a higher level than administrative assistant, given that she had already done that twice during previous jobs, and was tired of making phone calls and slide decks), but it was a start. A referral from a friend of a friend got her in the door, and, fortunately, she'd prepared with more mock interviews than she probably needed. But even entry level jobs were competitive, and Lacy did not take this one for granted. This was her chance to prove herself.

As she pushed through the glass doors of the sleek office building, she caught a glimpse of her reflection. She'd always been told she had a girl-next-door look, with her wavy, dirty-blonde hair, soft features, and an earnestness in her eyes that seemed to never fade. Today, she had tried to look like the young professional she hoped to be—her hair falling in perfect waves around her shoulders, her makeup minimal but polished, and her outfit carefully chosen to convey confidence and capability. That might be the only thing that went well today, but if so, at least she could tell she looked like she knew what she was doing.

Until she got to the security desk and had her first fumble of the day, not realizing she needed her ID to get into the building – all her interviews had been done remotely – and then not realizing she'd need a visitor's pass to activate the elevator. This all seemed a little extra to Lacy, and as she rode up to the 12th floor, she couldn't help but feel the flutter of compounded nerves in her stomach. She had spent years dreaming of escaping small town life and starting somewhere new, where she could define herself not as who everyone thought she was, but as who she wanted to be. Even during college, she still felt like she was same-old girl-next-door Lacy. She didn't even have a dorm, since she was living at home. But as much as she wanted to leave home, there were still parts of her past that she couldn't quite shake. Maybe being in the big city would help her put those past problems behind her.

The elevator doors opened to a hall, and she turned right to face... a wall. Lacy then turned around to face the doors leading to a bustling office space, open and modern with glass walls and bright, natural light streaming in through large windows. Lacy admittedly hated open offices. It felt intrusive to always be in everyone else's environment, and as an introvert, she would have preferred even cubicles to the long tables where everyone had their laptops set up. Her future coworkers were working - walking around, engaged in animated conversations or typing furiously at the table. It was a far cry from the quiet study sessions she used to have in her bedroom at home.

Lacy met a receptionist named Kathleen, who directed her to HR, where she met Darcy, who handed her a stack of paperwork and an office map. "Welcome to Carver, Lacy. You'll be assisting the creative department, and your direct supervisor, who's also starting with us today, is Melissa Brown. She's one of our account managers."

"Thank you," Lacy replied, trying to sound confident, despite the sudden jolt of nerves that hit her when she heard the name. Melissa Brown. It couldn't be, could it? She pushed the thought aside as she filled out her paperwork and handed over her ID once again. But memories lingered, and she had an uneasy feeling that the past she was trying to escape might be waiting for her in this building.

With her documents completed, Darcy took Lacy through the maze of tables, giving her a brief tour. The creative department was filled with people brainstorming ideas, sketching concepts, and discussing campaigns. This was where Lacy had hoped she might someday be, surrounded by creativity and innovation. She was admittedly surprised that a place specializing in selling cars could be quite so full of creative minds, and realized that she should probably drop her preconceived notions and try to start fresh here.

Darcy and Lacy stopped at a small office with a large glass wall that overlooked the city. In a way, Lacy was relieved that she hadn't been brought to those big tables. Maybe they'd give her a quiet space to work? "This is where you'll be working," Darcy said, gesturing to a desk just outside the office. *Still, better than those open tables.* "And this is Melissa's office. She should be here shortly, she's just checking in with Sophie, who runs creative."

"Great, thanks," Lacy said, trying to keep her voice steady, and with some amount of relief. At least she wouldn't be at one of those endless tables, surrounded by people. Having a little space of her own would mean she could get work done. She sat down at her new desk, logging on to her computer with the password Darcy had given her, as she tried to mentally prepare herself. It must be a coincidence. Melissa Brown was a common name. This wouldn't be the same Mel who had tutored her in math through her first three years of high school, her first real crush, who had shattered her heart on that fateful day at the end of junior year. Though, Mel didn't even know that any of that had happened. Lacy had never confessed her crush, or what she saw that day. She shoved those thoughts forcefully aside, determined to follow the mantra she had been taught: "leave your personal life outside the office."

But footsteps approached, and around the corner strode Melissa Brown. Lacy felt her heart stutter. It was her. Mel. *Remember to breathe, Lacy.* She breathed in and out, trying to calm her heart.

Mel was older now, but the years had only made her more striking. Her once long, sometimes mussed hair was styled in a sleek fade, and her wardrobe had shifted from the casual jeans and tank tops Lacy remembered to a tailored jacket, t-shirt, and dark washed jeans that exuded "creative, but still has her shit together." But her eyes—those bright, intelligent eyes that had always seemed to see right through Lacy—were the same. Mel had always been effortlessly cool, always seemed to have everything figured out, while Lacy had been the shy, awkward girl who never knew just what to say.

"Lacy?" Mel's voice was smooth, with a hint of surprise. "Is that you?"

Lacy stood, trying to find her voice. "Hi, Mel. I mean, Melissa? Do you go by Melissa now? I haven't seen you in a while, but the HR woman said Melissa, um, Darcy was her name? Anyway, so yeah, hi. Did you ask a question? I think you asked something, but now I've forgotten what you asked."

For a moment, Mel just looked at her, as if trying to reconcile the Lacy she had known with the (obviously nervous) woman standing in front of her. Then she smiled, that same easy smile that had always made Lacy's heart stop. "Wow, it's been a long time. I didn't expect to see you here. Small world, huh?"

"Yeah, for sure, small world," Lacy echoed, smiling too wide, then stopping herself from smiling, then trying to smile again, and when did smiling become such a difficult thing to do? *Pull it together, Lacy, dammit.*

"So, you're my assistant?" Mel asked, glancing at Lacy's desk. "Well, guess we'll both learn something on the job."

Lacy wasn't sure if she meant that in a good way or not, but she nodded. "I guess so."

As the conversation paused, Lacy's mind raced. She had spent so many years trying to forget about Mel, to bury the embarrassment of that day when she had shown up at Mel's place, heart pounding, ready to confess her feelings—only to find Mel kissing the captain of the football team. Lacy had been devastated, running away before they could see her, and had spent the rest of high school avoiding Mel entirely. She hadn't known that Mel was dating anyone, let alone someone like him. It had felt like a betrayal, even though she knew, deep down, that Mel hadn't owed her anything.

It's not like you were even out then, Lacy recalled, *at least not to Mel*. She'd come out the year after Mel left town, and while her small community hadn't been bothered, Lacy had wondered what life could have been like if the girl she was interested in dating knew about Lacy's feelings for her. But... Mel was straight, probably. Even with the kinda questionable haircut, Lacy knew you couldn't bank on how someone looked to define their sexuality, and even if Mel *was* possibly bi or pan or any kind of queer-who-might-like-girls, that didn't mean she would like Lacy. She probably saw Lacy as that kid she tutored, forever forgetting that $y = mx + b$.

So. Here they were, years later, thrown back together in the most unexpected way. Lacy couldn't help but wonder if Mel even remembered the end of that year, or if it had been just another moment in her effortlessly cool life – graduation had come so quickly on the heels of that day, and soon Mel was packing and off to college in the big city. This city, actually, now that Lacy had a moment to remember. But for Lacy, seeing Mel kissing Chet—of *course his name was Chet*, had been a defining moment—one that had shaped the way she approached relationships ever since. Or, more accurately, avoided them.

"Why don't we get you started?" Mel said, interrupting Lacy's thoughts. "We've got a big presentation in two weeks, and there's a lot to do."

"Sure," Lacy replied, trying to focus on the task at hand. She couldn't let herself get distracted by the past. This was her chance to prove herself, to show that she was capable and professional, even if it meant working alongside the one person she had never quite gotten over.

As the day went on, Lacy fell into the rhythm of the office. Mel was an efficient and demanding boss, but she was fair, offering guidance and feedback without ever making Lacy feel inadequate. They worked well together, their old familiarity making it easy to communicate and collaborate. But there was an undercurrent of tension, an unspoken history between them that neither of them acknowledged. Lacy wondered if Mel even noticed it was there at all.

It wasn't until later that evening, as Lacy was finishing up some last-minute tasks, that Mel finally broached the subject of the past. She leaned against the doorway of her office, watching Lacy with a curious expression. "So, Lacy, how have you been? It's been what, eight years?"

"Yeah, about that," Lacy replied, trying to keep her tone light. "I've been good. College, a few small jobs, then moved here. What about you?"

"Pretty much the same," Mel said with a shrug. "College, an entry level job at Prett, worked my way up to junior accounts over there, then landed this job. Life's been...busy."

There was a pause, and Lacy could feel the weight of things left unsaid. Finally, Mel sighed and crossed her arms. "Look, high school ended... abruptly. I don't know if there's anything you want to talk about there, and I know it was a long time ago, but...if you do, I'm here."

Lacy was caught off guard by the offer. She had never expected Mel to bring up the fact that Lacy had avoided her texts for weeks, till Mel stopped texting. But as much as part of her wanted to unload all the hurt and confusion she had carried for so long, another part of her wasn't ready.

"It's okay," Lacy said quietly, meeting Mel's gaze. "There's nothing to talk about."

Mel studied her for a moment, then nodded. "Alright. But if you change your mind, you know where to find me."

Lacy forced a smile. "Thanks, Mel."

As Mel walked back into her office, Lacy let out a breath she hadn't realized she'd been holding. Maybe it really didn't matter anymore. Maybe they could just work together, put the past behind them, and focus on the future.

But as she gathered her things and headed out of the office, Lacy couldn't shake the feeling that the past was far from over. And as much as she could try to convince herself otherwise, Lacy knew that working with Mel was going to be anything but simple. *If she'd only gotten less hot instead of growing up to be even hotter,* Lacy let her mind wander as she walked home.

She unlocked the door to her apartment and stepped inside, the quiet and simplicity of the space a stark contrast to the chaos of the city. She set her bag down and sank onto the futon she used as a couch-and-bed, staring out the window at the lights of the buildings across the street. She had worked so hard to get here, to build a new life.

Maybe Mel had been right. Maybe they did need to talk about what had happened all those years ago. But Lacy wasn't ready to have that conversation. Mel was her boss. Even if she ever *was* ready, it wasn't an appropriate conversation to have. Right now, Lacy should keep her focus on her job, on proving that she deserved to be here, working at the firm.

But even as she told herself that, Lacy knew it wasn't just about the job. It was about Mel, about the feelings she had buried for so long, and the possibility that maybe—just maybe—there could be a second chance waiting for her. *Stop thinking about her*, Lacy told herself, though she itched to run her hands along the freshly buzzed cut, to reach up, pull Mel down to her and—

No. Lacy stopped that thought in its very inappropriate tracks. That was cold shower thinking. She needed food, and sleep, and to get on with her life. In fact, she would do just that. She texted her best friend from college, Art, and gave him a brief rundown, mentioning the situation with Mel, as well as the stress and excitement of the new job. Art texted back a link to sign up for a dating app, and Lacy grimaced. She hated those things. And now was the time to focus on work. *If I do decide to date*, Lacy thought, *I'll download the app*. And then she could go out with someone and forget about Mel entirely. Which was really the best possible scenario for her dating life, anyway. Wasn't it?

Chapter 2: A Fresh Start, Indeed

Mel arrived at her desk early the next morning, ready and eager to get a jumpstart on her new role. Mel's new workspace was modest but functional—a small office with a door she could close for private calls and meetings. It was a far cry from the corner office she'd envisioned when she first dreamed of work in advertising, but only a few years in, she couldn't expect more than a place of her own, with a door to close. Didn't Virginia Woolf say you needed something like that? *Probably not*, Mel thought, *Lacy would know.*

That...was an unexpected thought to hit so early in the morning. But maybe not an entirely unwelcome one.

She had started at Carver the same day as Lacy Jennings, and they had both been thrown into the whirlwind of prepping for a presentation to one of the firm's mid-level clients. While Mel had hoped for a more experienced colleague, she appreciated knowing someone to share the initial chaos with. Though, neither had acknowledged their shared history publicly.

Would it be weird to? Mel wondered. She wasn't entirely sure of the office politics here, and while it might not be *that* strange to have a shared background with a coworker, she wasn't sure what the manager/ assistant relationship guidelines were. *I should ask Darcy*, she made a mental note to herself. It would be worth knowing, so she wouldn't seem overly familiar. *But what would overly familiar even be?* Mel wondered. Like... they could be friends, right? Did she want to be

Lacy's friend? Or something more? That...was an unexpected thought, even though it made Mel pause in reviewing her morning emails. Was she attracted to Lacy? Her nerdy but endearing mentee? Was that possible?

Mel had come out in college, though she'd known she was queer for most of childhood. She hadn't dated openly in high school. Aside from one misguided kiss with Chet, the football team captain who had chased her most of senior year, she had thrown her focus into college and her career. In college, she felt free to date, experimenting both romantically and sexually with other women. She learned the hard way that poly relationships were not her thing, and confirmed that she enjoyed sex with women, but hadn't found a real romantic relationship that lasted longer than a few months.

Mel had been trying to put high school out of her mind, given how much time she spent pretending to be something other than who she really was. She wanted to focus instead on her new responsibilities and the exciting challenges ahead. The firm had a reputation for excellence, and Mel was eager to prove herself. Her father's connections had helped her land this position, and she was determined to make the most of the opportunity, both for herself, and to justify her father's support.

As she continued reviewing her emails, she found her thoughts drifting again toward Lacy. The girl had always been smart and hardworking, but she seemed a bit overwhelmed by the sheer volume of work and fast pace of the office. It was clear she had potential, but she would need help to get up to speed. Mel wondered if she should take extra time to mentor Lacy here, too. Maybe they could go out for dinner. Or drinks. Or something that sounded less like a date.

Mel glanced at the clock and saw it was almost time for Lacy to arrive. She had been impressed with Lacy's enthusiasm to dive into the work the day before. It had been a whirlwind of introductions and briefings, and Mel was looking forward to helping her adjust to the demands of the job.

The office began to fill with morning buzz as more coworkers arrived, and Mel could hear the faint clinking of coffee mugs from the nearby kitchen. She was in the middle of responding to an email from a client who wanted to schedule a call about a major project milestone when Lacy walked in, looking more composed than the day before, in a blouse that hugged her curves in ways that made Mel flush involuntarily, betraying the calm mask she usually wore.

"Good morning, Lacy," Mel said, trying to cool herself down by looking back at her emails. "How are you today?"

"Hey, Mel," Lacy replied. "I'm good. Still working to get a handle on things."

"That's good to hear," Mel said, her heart beginning to resume its normal pace. *As long as I avoid looking at her, this will be fine. Jesus Christ, Mel, get it together.* "We have a lot to cover today. I thought we could start with a brief overview of the current accounts and then move on to getting the early draft of that presentation ready. How does that sound?"

"Sounds good," Lacy said, taking a seat at the desk just outside Mel's office. She sat down at her laptop, ready to take notes. Fortunately, she was just slightly out of sight, enough that Mel wouldn't catch sight of her just by glancing up. But they had to work closely together today, so Mel invited Lacy in to her office to look over their most important accounts.

Mel explained the details of ongoing campaigns, client preferences that she'd become aware of, and various internal processes to learn. Lacy was attentive and engaged, though Mel noticed that she had a tendency to drift off occasionally. It was something Mel had noticed during their studies together in high school. Possibly something she would need to address.

During a break, Mel saw Lacy texting someone. The sight was a bit distracting, but Mel chose not to comment, figuring it wasn't any of her business, even though she was curious to know who Lacy was talking to in the middle of the work day. Still, she could remember being in the same position not too long ago—learning the ropes while trying to juggle the demands of a new job.

Lacy's phone buzzed, and she glanced at the screen with a smile before quickly typing a response. Mel couldn't help but notice how the smile lingered on Lacy's face as she sent her message.

"Everything okay?" Mel asked, trying to sound casual.

"Oh, yeah," Lacy said, glancing up. "Just texting my friend. Art. He's coming to visit next Friday, so we're confirming plans. Oh—is it okay for me to text on work time? I don't want to get in trouble."

Mel's heart sank a little at the mention of Art. She had hoped to invite Lacy to dinner next Friday, to get to know her better outside of the office, but – she admitted to herself – the idea of this "Art" guy made her feel a little reticent to invite Lacy anywhere. She pushed the disappointment aside, forcing a smile. "That sounds nice. It's good to catch up with friends. And as long as you keep your work on schedule, it's fine to be sending a quick text now and then."

Lacy nodded, a puzzled expression at Mel's slight change in demeanor. But she went back to work on the presentation outline, and Mel returned to her office, though her mind kept drifting back to Lacy and the mention of Art.

As the day went on, Mel tried to focus. She had a few client calls and meetings scheduled, and she needed to stay on top of everything. Despite her best efforts, though, she couldn't shake the feeling that there was something more to Lacy's presence in her life than just a professional relationship.

Mel had come out midway through college. Her parents had been supportive, and she had navigated her relationships with confidence and clarity. But seeing Lacy stirred up feelings she wasn't prepared for.

It was odd, really—how could someone from her past become such an immediate focal point in her present?

She tried to keep her emotions in check. Mel knew she couldn't let whatever her personal feelings might be *and there can't possibly be personal feelings* interfere with her professional responsibilities. After all, their relationship had been strictly tutor and student, and it was important to maintain a professional demeanor.

As the end of the day approached, Mel called Lacy into her office to review the progress they had made. "You've done a great job today," Mel said, with a warm smile. "I can see you're getting the hang of things – the presentation outline is looking great, and we'll dive more into details tomorrow."

"Thank you," Lacy replied, looking genuinely pleased. "I appreciate your help. It's been a lot to take in, but I'm getting there."

Mel nodded, trying to ignore the pang of regret she felt about not having invited Lacy to that dinner. "I'm glad to hear that. If you need anything or have any questions, don't hesitate to ask. We're all learning together, and it's important to support each other."

"I will," Lacy said. "Thanks, Mel."

"And—" Mel started, then stopped, hesitant. Lacy's questioning look encouraged Mel to push forward. "I wondered if you might be interested in grabbing dinner—or lunch sometime. To catch up. Outside of work."

Obviously outside of work, you idiot, Mel thought, but tried to keep her expression neutral, in case Lacy turned her down.

"Definitely, yes!" Lacy seemed excited at the prospect, which made Mel smile. She remembered how excited Lacy got when she solved a math problem, and this seemed to align with her memories. *Well, at least I can confirm that I'm as exciting as finding the area of a triangle.*

"Great," said Mel, "I'll have my assistant set something up for us." She waited for Lacy to get the joke, and when Lacy laughed, Mel felt the warmth wash through her. *Worth it just for that.*

"I'll get it on our calendars," Lacy replied, sitting back at her desk.

"You don't have to do it right away," Mel chuckled.

"I want to," Lacy said, looking earnestly at her, and Mel nodded. She knew that look, too – the one that meant Lacy was trying hard, and that it meant something to her.

As Lacy finished scheduling their dinner (for Thursday, Mel noticed), she gathered her things and prepared to leave for the day. Mel watched with curiosity. She wanted to get to know Lacy better, to understand what had happened in their past. Why Lacy had shut her out at the end of senior year. *Lacy's junior year.* But she also wanted to respect the boundaries of their working relationship and avoid any complications. *Like the complication that you're apparently a giant horndog and need to stop lusting after your assistant.* Ugh. That was new. Maybe a cold shower and maybe some terrible reality TV would help her get over that feeling.

Lacy waved goodbye and walked out, leaving Mel alone with her thoughts. Mel sighed. She was beginning to worry that her feelings about Lacy might become more intense than she wanted them to be. Not that she wanted to have any feelings about Lacy at all.

Mel had always been driven by ambition and a desire to succeed, but now she found herself navigating not just the challenges of her career, but also the unexpected reappearance of someone who was taking more of her emotional energy than she thought possible.

She took a deep breath, trying to clear her mind. There was no need to overthink things. She had a job to do. Lacy was a smart and capable young woman, and Mel would help her succeed. Just as long as she kept things professional, everything would be fine. And there was nothing wrong with sharing a meal with a colleague. Even if their talk drifted towards their past, Mel could keep it in strictly friendly territory.

With one last glance at the city skyline, Mel left the office, determined to stop herself from thinking about her assistant, even if she might need more than a few episodes of bad TV to get through her feelings.

Chapter 3: Dinner.
Great.

Lacy appraised herself in the mirror, her heart definitely running faster than it should be as she adjusted the simple summer dress she'd picked out. She never got this nervous over a dinner with someone she knew, but this felt... different. Maybe it was because it was with Mel, her tutor. No, *Mel her boss.* But tonight was just about work, right? Mel surely only wanted to talk about the job, but still, it felt personal in a way she hadn't expected. The past few days, their conversations had remained professional, but Lacy felt a tension underneath it that she could have been imagining. But what if she wasn't imagining it?

Her phone buzzed, pulling her out of her thoughts. It was Art, already lounging on her couch.

Come out already, he texted. *I'm bored and the one photograph you have on the wall of that tree in your back yard is not interesting enough to keep looking at for another fifteen minutes.*

Lacy looked skyward, praying for sanity to a God she didn't believe in, before leaving her bathroom, counting as she walked.

"One Mississippi... two Mississippi..."

"Oh, good, you've learned your numbers." Art had his feet up on her couch and was scrolling his phone.

"I was just checking to see if it was really necessary to text me or if it was, in fact, two steps from my bathroom to my living room slash kitchen slash bedroom."

"Don't forget slash foyer slash sexytime room slash—"

"Shut up," Lacy stopped him. "There will be no sexytime while I'm out, young man."

"Maybe not for me, but you could get it in that dress," Art was appreciatively checking her out. Lacy knew he was being a good friend. He was head over heels in love with his fiancé Rob, but he still knew how to make a girl feel good about how she dressed.

"It's just dinner," Lacy said, but deep down, she knew it wasn't *just* dinner. It was dinner with Mel, the object of a crush that was once again rearing its head, no matter how much she tried to tamp it down. Her cheeks flushed as she attempted to ignore her feelings. "It's just a casual dinner to go over the proposal deck."

"Right. And you just happen to be turning red like you've been sitting in the sun for the last hour for a 'casual' work dinner with *Mellllll*," he teased, drawing the name out extra-long, giving her a smirk. "I know all your signs, lady. You're in looooooove."

Lacy froze for a split second before shaking her head. "No. I'm not. She's my boss now—junior account manager, actually. We're both new, and yes, it is weird seeing her again. But, you know, it's totally professional."

Art smirked. "Professional, sure. Just don't let that professionalism stop you from having a little fun. You told me about your long-time crush, and if she's anything like the pictures you've shown me—"

"That was high school," Lacy shot back, trying to laugh it off. "I was seventeen and didn't know anything."

"Uh-huh," Art replied, raising an eyebrow. "Well, she's here."

Lacy's phone buzzed, and Lacy's heart jumped. "How did you know that?"

"I heard someone in the hallway, and figured you didn't get a whole lot of visitors, seeing as you've been in the city for like all of twelve minutes."

Lacy smoothed the front of her dress and went to the door.

When she opened it, there was Mel, standing in the hallway with that easy smile, dressed casually—light jeans, a fitted gray sweater. It wasn't fancy, but Lacy found herself momentarily stunned by how good Mel looked, how at ease she seemed. There was something different about seeing her like this, outside the office. It felt both more comfortable and more complicated.

"Hey," Mel said, tone warm. "Ready?" Then she frowned, and Lacy returned a frown of her own, confused.

"Is everything okay?" Lacy asked.

"I didn't realize you had company," Mel said. "If you'd rather do this another night—"

"No, no," Lacy started, but was interrupted as Art rose from the couch and walked over.

"Artibald, I know it's a terrible name, my parents might have been going for Archibald, but they failed entirely, I go by Art, and I know, you're Lacy's boss Mel, and I'm just the visiting friend, here a day early. Don't worry, I've been to the city before, I know how to entertain myself while you two are out on the town. And you're both looking at me like I just ruined your favorite leather jacket—don't act like you both don't have one—and I did *no such thing.*" He stopped, and the two women looked at each other, a shared understanding: Art was cute, but it was time to go to dinner.

"Do a lot of things I wouldn't do," Lacy said, giving Art a peck on the cheek as she left.

"That list is a million items long, and I don't have nearly enough time to finish it!" Art called, as Lacy closed the door behind them.

As they stepped outside, the cool evening air hit her, and for a moment, Lacy felt more grounded, but then realized she didn't know where to put her hands. Pockets? Her dress had pockets, of course – but no, that was too casual. *Let them swing by your side, but not too much. Oh, God, why am I overthinking my hands?*

"So, Art seems nice," Mel said, breaking Lacy out of her thoughts.

"Yeah, we've known each other since college. His family moved to the area a little after you left, and of course he immediately became bffs with my dad."

"Why of course?" Mel looked unsure.

"You know, they're both big on sports and fixing cars," Lacy kept a straight face, waiting for Mel to get the joke.

"Into theater and he likes listening to NPR podcasts?" Mel asked.

"Nailed it," said Lacy. "Art and my dad are like two peas in an overly literate pod."

"It must make your parents happy to see you with someone like that," Mel said.

"With—ah—" Lacy wasn't sure how to answer that. Was Mel suggesting she and Art were together? That was ludicrous – Art was clearly gay, and Lacy was also gay, and *Mel probably doesn't know either of those things. Damn. How do I clear this up?*

But Mel had changed the subject, and Lacy's brain had to race to catch the topic. The pitch deck.

"Yeah, now that the outline's solid, I'm going to start working on getting those charts together in the next few days," Lacy promised.

"Great," said Mel. "Ask me for anything you need help on."

Despite the easy conversation, there was a current of something else between them, something unspoken that made Lacy feel oddly exposed.

"Do you go home much?" she asked, mentally kicking herself for changing the topic in a personal direction.

Mel smiled, but there was something behind it, a flicker of something unreadable. "Yeah, sometimes. It's weird being so far from where we grew up."

Lacy wondered how often Mel had been back, and why she'd never run into her. But, she'd been so busy with school, and then most of her off-hours were spent at home, studying. When Art did manage to drag her out, he always took her to the gay bar two towns over, and there's no way Mel would have ever been there, right? There was that one time Lacy swore she saw someone that looked like Mel making out with another girl during Lacy's sophomore year of college. But by the time she'd gotten the courage to walk closer, the two girls had left, holding hands. Lacy had been briefly heartbroken before convincing herself it wasn't Mel, couldn't possibly be Mel, Mel was straight, or if she wasn't straight, she was away at college and wouldn't be home, not even over a holiday weekend, which this was, but still.

They reached the small Thai restaurant Lacy had chosen, and her thoughts stopped wandering as Mel held the door open for her. The warmth and chatter of the restaurant greeted them as they stepped inside, the low lighting and the scent of ginger and garlic filling the space. The hostess led them to a small table near the window, and they settled into their seats.

For the first few minutes, they stuck to work—Mel had her tablet out, and they reviewed the proposal deck, the slides, and the target audience. Mel explained some of the ways to narrow down your demographics. As usual, she was laser-focused, her ideas sharp and on point. Lacy had always admired how quick and intuitive Mel was with her thinking, especially when it came to strategy. But as they talked, something tugged at Lacy's mind, something from their shared past.

"So, you think we should lead with the nostalgia angle?" Lacy asked, trying to pull herself back into the moment.

Mel thought for a moment. "I think it could work for the brand. They've been around for decades, so if we can tap into that emotional connection people already have, it could resonate," Mel replied, her voice calm and confident.

Lacy nodded, taking in what Mel said, but her mind was elsewhere. She couldn't stop thinking about their own shared past. The night she'd gone over to Mel's house at the end of junior year to...what? Confess? Confront her feelings? She still wasn't sure. But instead, she'd seen Mel with Chet. After that, she'd pulled back—stopped texting, stopped showing up for tutoring. She couldn't deal with it then, and she hadn't seen Mel since, until this job. At least, assuming that wasn't her at the bar that time. It couldn't have been, right?

She wondered if Mel remembered high school. Probably not. To Mel, she was just a kid from a small town, someone she'd tutored for extra cash. They were friendly, and they had had lunch sometimes, but that was just so they could eat while they studied. It wasn't like they were ever friends, not really.

As they finished their main course, they began reminiscing about the past—old friends, old hangouts, the way their town felt so far away now. They laughed about their high school's notoriously awful baseball team, the endless drama of small-town life, and how weird it was to run into people from home in the city.

"You remember Mrs. Walker, right?" Lacy asked, grinning. "She used to make us re-do every single math problem if we got even one wrong."

Mel chuckled. "How could I forget? I think she's half the reason I had to tutor you. She wasn't exactly the most forgiving."

Lacy smiled, feeling a strange sense of warmth at the shared memory. For a moment, it felt like they were back in that tiny town, just two girls navigating high school and homework. But then the warmth was tinged with something else—something she'd tried to bury for years.

She hesitated, the words on the tip of her tongue. Should she ask? Should she bring up that night, the reason she'd stopped talking to Mel all those years ago? Did Mel even remember?

Just as Lacy opened her mouth, Mel leaned forward slightly, her expression growing more serious. "Lacy, it might be out of line, but I've been meaning to ask—"

The waiter appeared suddenly, interrupting with the check. The moment evaporated, and Mel leaned back, her face shifting back into a more composed expression. She glanced at the bill, pulling out her wallet.

Lacy felt a pang of disappointment. *What did Mel want to ask?* But she could hardly push for it. The moment had passed.

Mel handed her card to the waiter and gave Lacy a smile that didn't quite reach her eyes as Lacy scrambled for her wallet. "Nope. I'm paying. I invited you. So, tomorrow, we should probably go over the mock-ups before the client meeting. I want to make sure we're on the same page, and you can ask any questions about what we're doing. Consider it a dry run for the bigger proposal next week."

"Yeah, of course," Lacy replied, forcing herself to focus on the task at hand. "I'll admit, I'm glad they pushed that one a week, so I have more time to work on the deck. I'll finish up the revisions on tomorrow's deck tonight."

"No," said Mel. "You have a guest. I'll do it. And I don't want you spending a lot of your off hours working. You should be enjoying the city, getting out with your boyfriend—"

"I don't have a boyfriend," Lacy said, stopping Mel. *Finally, an opening.*

Mel looked confused, "But Art—?"

"Art is gay," said Lacy, "As am I, too, also gay." *What in the world was that? Did I just come out in the most grammatically awkward sentence of all time? Was that even a sentence? A partial sentence. A phrase. I'm still thinking about this, and Mel hasn't responded.*

Mel's face was entirely unreadable, which made Lacy nervous. Had she said something she shouldn't? Was Mel—oh no, please no—homophobic?

"I didn't know," Mel said quietly, as if talking to herself more than to Lacy.

"Why would you? I never said anything," Lacy replied, her words a little more layered than she meant. *I never said anything, because I didn't know how to tell you without telling you I was in love with you.*

"So, ah- girlfriend, then," said Mel. "You should spend time out with your girlfriend, not sitting at home going over numbers."

"I—don't have one of those, either," said Lacy. "I'm single."

This seemed to surprise Mel more than the "I'm gay" revelation.

"You are?" A look Lacy had never seen in Mel's eyes before surfaced, before Mel shut down again, and Lacy wished she knew what that look meant. Mel's phone buzzed with a text, and she glanced down. The name of Mel's supervisor Sophie flashed across the screen, and Lacy knew Mel had to reply.

"Sorry, I'll just deal with this—"

They walked out of the restaurant as Mel texted. "I'm going to have to do some work sooner rather than later," said Mel. "I'd like to walk you home, but the subway—" she nodded to the stop at the corner.

"Sure, no problem," said Lucy, hesitating. "Do you need any help with the work...or?" Was this a hug goodbye moment? A kiss on the cheek? Something more? Less? How do you say goodbye to your boss who you totally still have a major crush on?

"I'm good, but thanks," said Mel.

Lucy leaned forward at the same time Mel did, and they both hesitated, lips inches away, before Mel shifted direction slightly, turning an almost-kiss into a quick hug.

"See you tomorrow, Lace," she murmured into Lacy's ear, and Lacy felt a shiver run through her whole body. She gasped, probably audibly judging from the question in Mel's eyes, but Lacy turned and walked back to her apartment before anything more could be said.

Art was waiting for her on the couch, as if nothing had changed – aside from the Italian takeout he was devouring, while streaming one of his favorite shows on his laptop.

Lacy couldn't shake the feeling that she'd come close to something—some conversation or realization—that neither she nor Mel was quite ready to face. There was something between them now. Something more than just a friendship or just a boss/assistant relationship. But what it was, she didn't know. And for now, maybe it was better that way.

As Lacy sat down next to Art to recount her evening, she couldn't help but wonder what Mel had been about to ask before the waiter brought the check—and why part of her was glad she hadn't asked.

Chapter 4: An Art-istic Interpretation

Lacy leaned back against the cushions of her couch, her mind swirling with everything that had happened over dinner. Art, sitting cross-legged at the other end of the couch, was halfway through his second beer (well, third if you count the one he drank before she got back) and waiting for the rundown.

"So..." he said, nudging her with his foot. "Do I have to ask, or should we just do the 'you stare into space and think about it and I guess what you're thinking' thing?"

Lacy gave a half-smile. "I would like to pick whatever is behind door number three, please."

Art raised an eyebrow. "Door number three is a toaster oven, and you already have one of those."

"I do. And it works, too."

Art shook his head. "Tell me before I have to beg pathetically."

Lacy exhaled slowly, debating how much to say. She glanced over at Art, who had that expectant look on his face—that always reminded her why he made such a good listener. He'd come into her life well after her high school days were behind her, and knew basically everything about her past and that traumatic day that she was still *trying* to forget, but still *couldn't* forget.

"Well," she started, "We talked about the deck proposal we're working on. Went over some key points for the pitch, like how we can tie the product's brand story to the target audience's lifestyle. You know, usual boring advertising stuff."

"Shut up, you love advertising." Art gave her a look that said, *cut to the chase.*

Lacy grinned. "I do."

"Annnnnd then you made out and shocked the entire restaurant with all the kissing?"

Lacy grimaced. "And then we caught up on some personal stuff. She asked about college, my family, you know, that kind of thing. And it was... strange."

"Strange how?"

"Because, you know," she said, folding her hands in her lap. "We spent a lot of time together, and then...I just stopped talking to her. I never told her why. I don't even know if she noticed or cared, but now we're working together, and it's like the past is sitting right there between us."

Art nodded. "Okay, so I have the basic gist of what went down, but you really just ghosted her? Like flat-out no contact?"

Lacy shrugged. "I didn't know how to handle it at the time. I'm not sure I know how to handle it now."

Art took a swig of beer, brow furrowed. "Did you at least talk about why you stopped talking back then?"

"She didn't bring it up, and wasn't about to," Lacy shuddered at the thought. "But there was this moment...I think she was going to ask...something. Maybe about that." Lacy stared at the ceiling, her voice barely above a whisper. "I just felt everything I'd tried to forget was coming back. But then the waiter interrupted, and the conversation just...dropped. You know, I'm probably overthinking it. I'm sure she just wanted to ask about schedules or something..."

Art put down his empty bottle and reached for another one. Lacy smacked his hand. "Three is enough, young man."

Art looked wounded, but agreed. "I do have to be up early to give myself a tour of the city while you go to work with Hot High School Lady. Actually, I need to workshop that nickname. Maybe that's what I'll do tomorrow."

Lacy nodded wisely. "At least you have plans to be useful to the world."

"Yes, I am both useful to the world and helpful to my friends. So, when are you going to talk to Hottie McHighSchool about what happened? Nope, still a bad nickname

Lacy blinked. "The nickname is awful, but I am *not* about to bring this stuff up with her."

"I mean, you have some unresolved stuff here. Are you going to let it sit there, or are you going to deal with it?"

Lacy sat up a little straighter, her arms crossing defensively. "It's not like that. I'm her assistant. I have to be professional. Whatever happened in high school doesn't matter anymore."

Art rolled his eyes—an exaggerated gesture that made Lacy smile, despite present uncertainties. "Professional or not, you two have history. And we all know this whole thing is going to give you an ulcer if you don't address it."

She ran a hand through her hair. "I don't even know how to start that conversation without it sounding weird. What do I say, 'Hey, remember that time I ghosted you without an explanation? Wanna run through those details, maybe between working on this deck outline and the next client meeting?'"

Art grinned. "I think...no. But Lace, if this is bothering you, you've got to find a way to bring it up. You know how you get when you internalize everything and then years later you run into your high school crush and you don't even know how to have a conversation about how you feel."

Lacy leaned her head back. "Art. You cannot use the thing you're referring to as a metaphor for the thing you're referring to.

Art shrugged. "I can do what I want, you're not my mom."

Lacy leaned her head back, staring at the ceiling again. "I just...don't want to make things awkward. And, honestly...I think part of me is scared of what she'll say."

Art studied her for a moment. "Scared? Why?"

Lacy swallowed, her voice barely above a whisper. "Because—I just don't want another straight woman crush situation. Remember what happened sophomore year?"

Art nodded. "Kaila Hoover."

Lacy said, "Yeah. We are not relitigating that, don't worry. Just—seeing Kaila kissing a guy outside Benson Hall did not make me more likely to take risks on straight women."

Art shifted closer. "Okay, first of all, I saw the way she looked at you when she came to pick you up. There's something there that's more than just a straight woman and her assistant. Trust me."

Lacy shook her head slowly. "Art, that's just you projecting."

"I'm not projecting! I have instincts, and my instincts say there's something going on between you two. You might not be able to see it from inside your beautiful head, but it's there."

Lacy refused to let herself go down that path. "It doesn't matter. Even if there is something there, and I'm not agreeing that there is, it would be so unprofessional. What if something did happen and she lost her job?"

Art let his grin grow back. "So, you're open to the idea of something happening?"

"That's not what I said, and you know it."

Art didn't press her further. Instead, he redirected the conversation, "So, what's she like now, anyway? Outside work stuff, I mean."

Lacy relaxed a little. "She's pretty much the same. Sharp, confident, and still somehow, like, always the coolest person in the room. It's annoying, really."

Art's eyes lit up. "Annoying or...something else?"

"*Art*," she warned.

"Okay, okay," he threw up his hands in surrender. "I'm just saying. I think this whole thing is more two-sided than you're willing to admit."

Lacy didn't respond, her thoughts drifting back to dinner, to the easy conversation, and the way Mel had hesitated right before the waiter interrupted them. What had she been about to ask?

Whatever it was, Lacy wasn't sure she was ready to find out.

Chapter 5: Missed Signals

Mel strode down the hallway, heading toward Sophie's office. Most people hadn't arrived yet, but that's exactly how Sophie liked to work—early, focused, uninterrupted. Mel had reviewed the proposal deck a few times, and though she was confident, she always felt the need to prepare just a little more when dealing with Sophie.

Sophie was not just her supervisor. In the short time since they'd started working together, she had become a mentor—someone who had an easy command of the room, and someone Mel admired deeply. Her confidence made her both inspiring and, to some degree, intimidating. Mel knew that most of the junior staff, including Lacy, felt that way about Sophie, too.

Mel reached Sophie's door. Mel bypassed the assistant's empty desk and knocked. She heard the call from inside, "Come in!"

Opening the door, Mel stepped into Sophie's meticulously organized office. The walls were lined with books on marketing strategy, behavioral economics, and even leadership theory, all organized by topic and color. It was a nice aesthetic, even though Mel preferred alphabetic order, herself. The scent of Sophie's ever-present lavender diffuser filled the room, calming and sharp.

"Morning," Sophie greeted with a smile, gesturing toward the chair opposite her desk. "You're early."

"Morning," Mel returned the smile as she took her seat. "Wanted to go over the deck before we meet with the client."

Sophie nodded, glancing at the tablet in front of her, where the proposal was already open. "I went through it last night. It's strong. But we should tighten up the messaging on the brand's customer journey. They want to stand out, but we don't want to overwhelm them with jargon. Let's make it clear and relatable. And cut down the number of words on slide three and five, they're too busy."

Mel nodded, taking notes. "Got it. I'll simplify. I was thinking we could emphasize their connection with consumers emotionally, especially in the digital campaign."

"Exactly." Sophie leaned back in her chair, eyes narrowing slightly as she studied Mel. "But before we dive too deep into the deck, I wanted to check in on something."

Mel felt her nerves activate and met Sophie's gaze, waiting. She could stay calm in front of authority, but it was always worrisome to be questioned by her boss, even if it didn't turn out to be a big deal.

"How's it going with your assistant?" Sophie asked, her tone casual but her expression serious. "Lacy, right? I know she's pretty new to the ad world. How's she handling things?"

Mel tensed. The question was innocent on the surface, but she'd been expecting it—or something like it—to come up eventually. Sophie knew they were from the same small town, though Mel hadn't gone into any detail about their past beyond that. She'd just been Lacy's tutor, nothing more. Despite her confused feelings. *Which are totally fine and not at all a problem*, she reminded herself.

"Lacy's great," Mel said, keeping her tone neutral. "Still learning the ropes, but she's smart and eager. I think she'll get the hang of everything soon."

Sophie tilted her head, a faint smile playing at the edges of her lips. "That's good to hear. But you two knew each other before, right? You both come from, where is it?"

Mel's stomach tightened. "Small-town Colorado. Yeah. I was her math tutor in high school. We weren't, like, close or anything—just part of the same school."

Sophie raised an eyebrow, the faint smile lingering. "Is it strange to be her supervisor, given the old connection?"

Mel forced a chuckle, hoping it sounded casual. "Not really. I mean, we hadn't spoken in years before she started here. It was just a tutor-mentee thing. Nothing major."

Sophie's gaze lingered for a moment longer, and Mel had the distinct impression that Sophie could see straight through her. It was a skill Sophie had—reading people, picking up on what they didn't say.

"And there's nothing else there?" Sophie asked, tone casual but eyes sharp. "No old feelings or tension? I've been hearing good things about both of you. I want to make sure you're comfortable with the setup."

Mel swallowed, trying to keep her expression neutral. "No, nothing like that. I mean, look. She doesn't even know this, and it's totally irrelevant, but yeah, I thought she was cute back then, but it was high school. I didn't even really know myself then. It was just...a phase, I guess."

Sophie's smile widened slightly, expression still annoyingly unreadable. "Well, just be careful. You're her supervisor now, and feelings could change the dynamic. If there's any potential for a conflict of interest, we need to address it early."

Mel blinked, caught off guard. "You think there might be a conflict of interest? I wouldn't want to do anything against policy."

Sophie shrugged. "Not yet. But, look. It's none of my business, but I'm intuitive enough to know that there could be something more going on there. I've seen the way she looks at you."

This was a revelation to Mel, who was totally caught off-guard. "The way she looks at *me*?"

Sophie nodded. "It could just be a hero worship thing, or an assistant admiring her boss thing, but it could be...more. There are some tricky things to get around, given the supervisor/assistant situation. If you find you want to explore something more personal, we need to put some distance between you. We don't have a strict policy against people dating their coworkers. But if it's between a supervisor and a subordinate, things get iffy. If something seems to be crossing the line, let me know, and we can talk about transferring one of you to another team. That's not a slight on you, by the way—you two seem to be working well together. I just don't want anything to become a problem that doesn't need to be. And your personal business is your own, until it risks internal policy."

Mel felt a rush of discomfort. She was a professional, and Lacy was her assistant. That was all. But the conversation with Sophie was forcing her to confront something she hadn't been ready to openly admit, even to herself.

"I don't think it's going to be an issue," Mel said, her voice a little too tight. "Like I said, it was a high school crush. She didn't even know I'm gay. Or, maybe still doesn't. And I'm over it."

Sophie raised an eyebrow. "Okay. Just keep me posted. None of this is bad, Mel. Not at this point. We'll figure it out."

Mel nodded, feeling the weight of the conversation settling on her shoulders. She glanced down at her notes, trying to refocus on the task at hand, but her mind kept wandering back to Lacy. The way she had smiled during dinner last night, the ease with which they had slipped back into conversation about their hometown, the brief flicker of something unspoken between them.

Was she really over it?

"Anyway," Sophie said, standing up and smoothing her blazer, "Let's get back to the deck. We've got the client in thirty minutes."

Mel snapped back to attention, standing up as well. "Right. I'll make those tweaks you mentioned beforehand."

Sophie nodded, her professional demeanor snapping back into place. "Good. And Mel—" she shifted to a more personal tone,

"Remember, you don't have to handle everything on your own. If things get complicated, talk to me."

Mel offered a tight smile. "I will. Thanks, Sophie."

Mel left Sophie's office, the weight of their conversation lingering. As she headed back to her desk, her phone buzzed, and she glanced at it to see a text from Lacy.

Lacy: Just finished those edits you asked for on the deck! Sending it over now.

Mel stared at the message for a moment, her mind swirling with everything Sophie had just said. She typed back a quick reply:

Mel: Thanks. See you in the meeting.

Returning to her own office, she passed Lacy's desk and stopped to say something, then noticed Lacy texting Art, and decided against it. She returned to her own desk, set her phone down and stared at the deck on her screen. The work was piling up, and she had no time to waste with distractions. But the more she tried to focus, the more her thoughts drifted back to Lacy.

Maybe Sophie was right.

Maybe there was something she needed to address, after all.

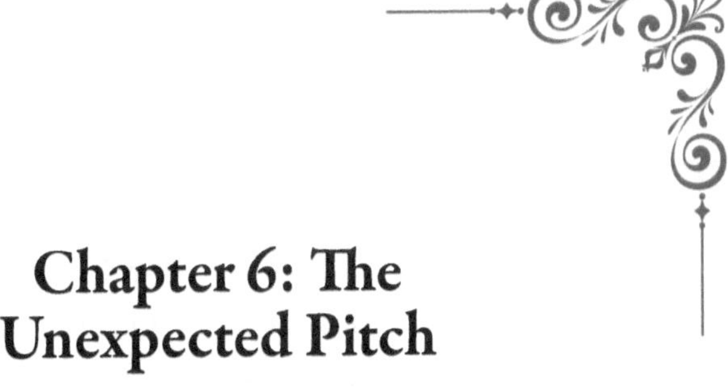

Chapter 6: The Unexpected Pitch

Lacy stared at her screen, reviewing the final tweaks on the deck she'd just sent to Mel. She had stayed up late the night before making sure everything was perfect—making sure the fonts were consistent, adjusting the layout, tightening the language. When the last email with the edited slides finally left her inbox, she felt a hint of pride. This was good work. Clean. Creative. Ready. And with Mel's guidance, she was sure she'd knocked it out of the park.

She leaned back in her chair, stealing a glance at the clock on her computer screen. Ten minutes until the meeting. Just enough time for a coffee.

As she stood up, she noticed Mel through the narrow glass window of her office door, sitting at her desk, probably checking through the most recent changes Lacy had sent over. Lacy couldn't help but smile. Mel always compelled her, even when she was clearly in the middle of handling a dozen different tasks. It reminded her of high school, how focused Mel had been while tutoring her in math, always having the answer, always calmly talking her way through figuring out the solution to the problem.

She grabbed her coffee mug and was about to head to the kitchen, when she noticed something odd. Mel was still at her desk, but instead of nodding approvingly, Mel's fingers were moving across her keyboard, making quick changes.

Wait.

Lacy's stomach twisted.

Was Mel...changing her work? Now?

Lacy quickly sat back down, her coffee mug forgotten. Maybe Mel was working on something else. Another project? She clicked over to the shared document Mel had just updated and felt her heart sink. Some of the design tweaks she had spent hours perfecting were gone. The polished transitions, the bold callouts, even some of the phrasing she'd worked so hard to get right—erased or modified.

Her breath caught in her throat. Why would Mel do that?

A quick scan through the deck confirmed it: Mel had overridden her changes. And not just small edits—major ones. Even the concept had shifted. These kinds of changes made it look like Lacy hadn't done half the work she had actually done.

Lacy's fingers hovered over her keyboard, ready to type a message, ready to ask Mel why she had changed so much at the last minute. But...she hesitated. She didn't want to sound ungrateful, or worse, defensive. What if Mel thought she was questioning her authority? Maybe Mel was just cleaning things up, because she knew the client better than Lacy did. But how was that possible, when they'd been there for the same amount of time, working so closely together? Lacy chewed the inside of her cheek, feeling tension rise in her chest.

Maybe she had misunderstood something. Maybe she hadn't gotten the brief as clear as she thought. But Mel had approved most of her work the night before...hadn't she?

Lacy clicked through the deck again, feeling a mix of confusion and frustration. This was a complete override of her work. Her confidence, which had been so high when she sent the final version, crumbled. Had she done something wrong? Was her work not up to Mel's standards?

The door to Mel's office opened, and Lacy minimized the deck, pretending to be busy with checking through some metrics Mel wanted her to review. Mel stepped out, her expression focused, a tablet tucked under her arm.

"Ready for the meeting?" Mel asked, her voice as calm as usual, but Lacy couldn't help but detect a hint of something else—maybe tension. Or was it nerves?

Lacy nodded quickly, forcing a smile. "Yeah."

Something about the way Mel glanced back at Lacy made her stomach twist again. Did Mel know how much Lacy had poured into the deck? Did she even care?

The walk to the conference room felt longer than usual. Mel was in front, Lacy trailing a few steps behind, her mind racing with a dozen different questions. Should she bring it up? Should she ask why Mel had changed so much? Maybe Mel had gotten feedback from someone higher up...but wouldn't she have told Lacy first? Wasn't that what good managers did—communicate?

The conference room was filling up when they arrived. Sophie was seated at the head of the table, scrolling through her tablet, and a few other team members set up laptops. Lacy found a seat off to the side, while Mel took her place closer to Sophie, naturally fitting to the rhythm of the account manager.

Lacy's heart pounded as she watched the client's representative—a middle-aged man with an expensive suit and an air of quiet authority—enter the room. He nodded to everyone as he took his seat, his assistant setting up beside him.

"All set?" Sophie asked, glancing at Mel.

"Good to go," Mel replied smoothly, not a trace of worry in her voice.

Lacy clenched her fists under the table. *She didn't even mention the last-minute changes?* Well, maybe she wouldn't have wanted to in front of a major client. But, still...it felt wrong.

As the presentation began, Lacy felt herself slipping further and further into the background. Mel was doing a great job—but Lacy couldn't stop thinking about the deck. The version they were presenting was polished, sure, but it wasn't the version she had spent hours perfecting.

Halfway through the pitch, Mel pulled up one of the slides Lacy had originally designed. It was one of the ones Mel had changed the most—replacing Lacy's clean, minimalist layout with something bolder, with more color and a heavier emphasis on statistics. The client nodded approvingly, jotting down notes, while Lacy felt a pang of disappointment.

Maybe Mel was right to change it. The client seemed to like it. But that didn't make Lacy feel better.

She stole a glance at Mel, who was confidently walking the room through the next phase of the campaign. Mel commanded attention, even in a room full of people with more experience. It reminded Lacy of why she had looked up to her so much in high school. But now, that admiration was mixed with something else: frustration.

As the meeting wrapped up, the client thanked them for their work, praising the team for their insights. Everyone smiled and shook hands, and for a moment, Lacy allowed herself to feel proud of being part of the team. But as soon as the room began to empty, the tension returned.

Mel packed up her tablet, and for the first time since the meeting started, she glanced over at Lacy. "Hey, good job on the prep," she said quietly. "I know I changed some things last minute, but I didn't have time to explain before the meeting."

Lacy swallowed hard, trying to keep her voice steady. "I noticed." She left it there, deciding not to press the point. If Mel wanted to explain, she would.

Mel gave her a small, apologetic smile. "It wasn't about your work. It's solid, Lacy. Sophie and I just had a quick talk this morning, and we decided to shift the focus. It was a timing thing, not a reflection on you."

Lacy nodded slowly, though the explanation didn't make her feel much better. She wanted to believe Mel—that it wasn't about her, that her work was still valued. But part of her still felt sidelined, like she was playing a supporting role in a project she had poured her heart into.

"Sure," Lacy said finally, pretending not to care. "Got it."

Mel looked like she wanted to say more, but Sophie's voice cut through the moment as she called across the room, "Mel, can I grab you for a quick debrief?"

"Absolutely," Mel replied, glancing back at Lacy one last time. "Let's talk more later, okay?"

Lacy forced a smile and nodded, not trusting her voice to sound totally honest if she responded.

As Mel walked away, Lacy stood there for a moment, watching her go. She didn't know why this was bothering her so much. Mel was her boss, not her tutor. They were in the real world; changes happened. That was part of the job.

So, why did it feel so personal?

Lacy sighed and started gathering her things, her mind spinning with questions. She wanted to be good at this—to prove herself. But right now, all she could think about was the way Mel had quietly rewritten and reformatted nearly all her work without even telling her. Would it have taken more than a few seconds to let Lacy in on the changes—maybe even let her help with the updates?

As she left the conference room and headed back to her desk, her phone buzzed in her pocket. She pulled it out, hoping for a message from Mel. But it wasn't. *Of course not. Mel's in a meeting with Sophie.*

It was Art.

Art: How was the big pitch? On a scale of 1 to Hot Boss Makes Out With Me In Front of Client?

Lacy smiled despite herself, typing a quick response.

Lacy: It was fine. And shut up. But.... Yeah. It was fine. Let's just drink tonight, okay?

Art: Ruh-roh, that doesn't sound like "fine" to me.

Lacy: I'll figure it out, Art. Just...drinks later.

Art: Yesssss. Driiiiiinks.

Lacy stared at the screen for a moment longer, then slipped the phone back into her pocket. Maybe Art was right. She just needed to figure things out. Were they on some kind of equal ground—personally *or* professionally? With mixed signals coming from Mel, Lacy wasn't sure where to start.

Chapter 7: Out of Focus

Mel stared at the debrief notes from the earlier client meeting, pen in hand, underlining key points as she mentally went over her next steps. The meeting with the long-term client had gone well, but it was kind of a softball meeting: they knew what the client would want in advance, based on prior interactions and previous notes in the lead-up to the presentation. The real challenge lay ahead: prepping for the pitch with the potential new client next week.

This one was different—more difficult to sell, but in some ways easier. There were no existing expectations to navigate, no patterns to uphold. Everything was on the table, and they could shape the pitch however they wanted. The blank slate was both an opportunity and a risk. Mel had to be sure the team nailed it on the first attempt, which could make or break her time at Carver.

She skimmed Sophie's notes from the post-meeting debrief, taking care to update a document she kept with areas that needed further attention. She liked to keep track of personal feedback, so she would know how to make adjustments going forward. In this case, messaging was going to be critical. The new client—an up-and-coming company breaking into the wellness space—would need a fresh, compelling narrative to differentiate them in an oversaturated market.

"You did a great job in the last meeting. I'd like us to keep a similar angle. Focus on the emotional hook," Sophie had said during the debrief. "They want data, but don't bog them down with numbers—they want to make an impact through their story. They also have money to burn, so we want to make sure it seems like we're targeting the right budget for them to make an impact. This is all about their identity, their brand voice, *who* they want to be seen as."

Mel chewed on the end of her pen, thoughts swirling around the challenge ahead. It wasn't that this new client was hard to crack; it was more that they had a vision so big it could easily overwhelm the team. Narrowing it down would take skill, precision, and collaboration. And then she couldn't help repeating Sophie's phrase in her head—who the client wanted to be seen as. But who did she, Mel, want to be seen as? Was she the buttoned-up boss, or the high school tutor, or...why did these tangents always lead back to Lacy? She was going to have to talk to her therapist about this, at some point, because it was clearly getting in the way of work.

Shaking herself out of her reverie, she mentally outlined how she would handle the proposal. First, the tone had to shift from formal to personable. Then, the visuals—bright, pleasing, but not over-the-top. This wasn't about being flashy; it was about crafting a brand people could trust.

Satisfied with the plan, Mel jotted down her main ideas and leaned back in her chair. She glanced at the clock. Still plenty of time before she needed to meet with Sophie again to review strategy.

But as her eyes drifted from her notes, her thoughts followed suit—shifting from the upcoming pitch to Lacy, the silence between them gnawing at her.

Lacy had been noticeably cold since the meeting earlier in the day. Mel knew why, of course. It was always tough to be a new assistant and be excited about your project, only to have your ideas overridden by someone else. But, she hadn't had time to explain; Lacy could have asked questions, but seemed to just accept the changes as a necessity, even though she was clearly upset. The changes Mel had made to Lacy's proposal slides—while necessary—had stung more than expected. It was clear in Lacy's clipped responses, the way she avoided eye contact.

Mel sighed, pressing her palms to her eyes. She should have anticipated this. Lacy had put in a lot of work, and even if it was a small change, it probably felt like a major criticism. When Mel was starting out, she would've been just as frustrated. She recalled one such assignment she'd done that got completely thrown in the trash before a meeting with the client. Mel had shortly moved to a new firm, and while she'd left because of the pay (or, she told herself that's why she'd left), she knew that part of her search for a new job was due to feeling like she wasn't respected by her superiors. But it wasn't as if Mel didn't trust Lacy's judgment. She was simply acting on Sophie's orders, sticking to guidelines that the client sent over at the last minute.

But there was no way Lacy could know that—and that was very much Mel's fault.

The distance between them had grown over the past few hours, stretching wider with each passing minute. Mel missed the easy connection they'd shared, even that morning. Now, it felt as if there was an invisible wall between them.

She sat up straighter in her chair, trying to angle her chair to get a glimpse of where Lacy sat. The younger woman was focused on her computer, buried in spreadsheets. Her demeanor was unreadable—another stark contrast to the usual energetic impression she exuded.

It stung, seeing her closed down.

Mel frowned, her mind wrestling with the best approach. She needed to say something. Or should she just give it space? *No,* she thought *I need her to be okay with me. I need us to be okay.* Maybe it wasn't such a big deal to Lacy, and maybe Mel was overthinking it—but what if she wasn't? What if this unresolved tension got worse, affecting their work together?

Mel tapped her pen on her desk, trying to find the right words. She had to make sure they were okay—both for their working relationship and for...well, for whatever else there might be between them.

Sighing, she got up and crossed the office to Lacy's desk, sitting on the edge of it, facing Lacy. She suddenly realized this was a bad idea as she followed Lacy's gaze, which was not at eye level, but instead began at Mel's legs. Lacy's eyes ran over Mel's body with a look that Mel had never seen in her before. She liked it; but it also frightened her, and what if she was misreading everything?

"Hey," she said softly, breaking Lacy's reverie, trying to sound upbeat despite the awkwardness in the air. "Can you come in to my office for a minute?"

Lacy didn't immediately look up from her screen. When she did, her expression was tight, her usual warmth missing.

"Fine," Lacy said, her tone clipped. "I'll just finish these reports."

She followed Mel into the office, and Mel asked her to close the door, sitting back behind her desk. She hoped in the more private space, the tension would ease. It didn't.

"Actually, I was thinking, maybe after work, we could grab a drink or something? Talk about the next few weeks of work, see where we want to take things."

For a moment, Lacy hesitated, eyes cast down. Her gaze flickered to Mel before darting away. "I... have plans tonight."

"Oh," Mel said, doing her best to keep the disappointment out of her voice. "What's up?"

"Art," Lacy said, her tone neutral. "He's only in town for a little while longer, so we're going out."

Mel blinked, her chest tightening slightly. She had forgotten Lacy had a friend in town. Entirely her fault. *Fine. If she's going out, I'm going out.* "Got it. Well... have fun."

Lacy nodded but didn't offer anything more. She was already returning to her work, making it clear the conversation was over.

Mel leaned back in her chair, a heaviness settling over her. She had no right to be bothered by Lacy's plans—despite their past, they were just colleagues. But the coldness in Lacy's voice, the way she kept her distance, made it clear there was something bad hanging between them.

For the rest of the afternoon, the silence deepened. Every time Mel looked, Lacy was lost in her work, her face expressionless. It was unlike her to be so distant. But Mel didn't know how to fix it. She knew why Lacy was upset, but it didn't feel like something that could be addressed beyond what she'd already said, and Lacy was clearly not interested in spending time together outside the office. She tried to remember what her own prior bosses had done when she was upset, but came up blank.

By the time five o'clock rolled around, Mel was more than ready to leave, though the tension hadn't let up. She grabbed her bag, watching as Lacy packed up her things at her own desk. There were so many words Mel wanted to say—apologies, questions—but nothing felt right.

As they walked to the elevator together, the silence somehow got heavier. Mel's thoughts churned as she tried to find a way to break it.

"Have fun with Art tonight," she said finally, hoping to at least bridge the gap before the weekend.

"Thanks," Lacy replied, her voice still closed down.

They got on the elevator together, and Mel pressed the lobby button, her fingers accidentally brushing the front of Lacy's blouse.

It was so subtle that, for a moment, it seemed like nothing. But then, just as Mel felt like maybe –maybe they could both pretend it hadn't happened—Lacy inhaled sharply, her breath catching, and Mel's hand hesitated just a fraction too long before she pulled away.

The warmth of the touch left a trail of electricity between them, a charge neither could ignore.

Their eyes met, and the air in the small space thickened. Mel's heart pounded in her chest, her pulse quickening. Lacy's expression was unreadable, her lips slightly parted, her gaze locked on Mel's with a mix of confusion and something else—something deeper. *But, no...*Mel thought, hopelessly, helplessly...*She can't possibly feel that way about me.*

Neither of them spoke. The silence wasn't uncomfortable, but charged with an electricity that hadn't been there before. Mel swallowed, her mouth dry, her hand now resting by her side, every inch of her aware of Lacy's presence nearby. Mel took a step back, creating physical distance, in case—in case what? In case Lacy's angry? But that look in her eyes is anything but anger.

Lacy's eyes flickered down briefly, then back up to meet Mel's, as if searching for an explanation. But there was none—at least not one that either of them was willing to say out loud.

Instead, they stood there, the unspoken weight of their history, proximity, and feelings pressing in around them. It was as if they were on the edge of something, teetering between what had always been and what could be.

Mel was about to say something, to break the interminable silence, when the elevator jolted beneath their feet.

Her hand flew to the railing for balance, her eyes meeting Lacy's wide, startled ones.

"Did the elevator just... stop?"

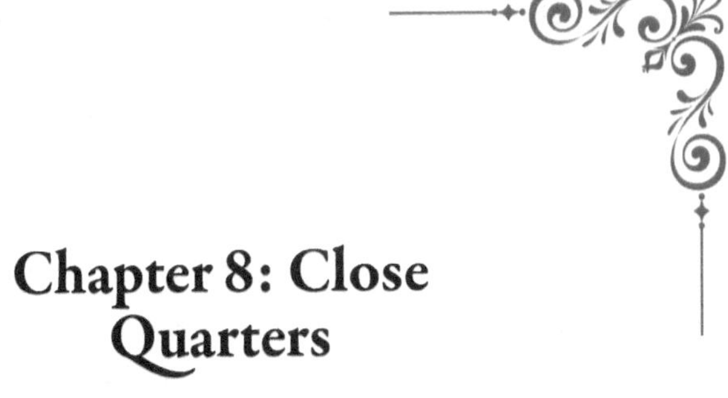

Chapter 8: Close Quarters

The elevator came to a sudden, jarring halt, sending a sharp groan through the cables overhead. Mel's hand shot to the control panel, her finger pressing the button for their floor, then the lobby, as if that would magically fix the problem.

Nothing happened. The elevator stayed still.

"Nothing works?" Lacy's voice was almost hesitant, like she was hoping Mel would fix this all, somehow.

Mel's jaw clenched, her usual composure visibly strained. Then, she pressed the help button. The intercom crackled to life after a pause.

"We're aware of the issue with your elevator," a tinny voice said. "Maintenance is on the way. Shouldn't be too long."

"How long is 'not too long'?" Lacy asked, her voice sharper than she intended.

"We'll get you out soon. Hang tight." And with that, the line went dead.

Mel exhaled slowly, still staring at the buttons, and for the first time since Lacy had known her, she seemed...rattled. It wasn't much, but there was a shift in her demeanor, something more fragile underneath that usual cool exterior.

Lacy leaned back against the elevator wall, trying to gauge how serious Mel's discomfort was. "Are you...okay?"

Mel nodded stiffly. "Fine. I just...don't love small spaces."

The admission took Lacy by surprise. Mel was claustrophobic? It didn't fit the image of her friend-turned-boss, always so poised, so put-together. Lacy had never seen her anything but calm, even under stressful circumstances. But right now, that mask was cracking.

"Oh. Okay. I get that," Lacy said, trying to sound casual, but the energy in the elevator was palpable. She shifted on her feet, glancing up at the floor display again, as if staring at the frozen numbers would somehow make them move. She didn't have claustrophobia, but she had enough anxiety about other things to have a sense of how Mel was feeling. Especially recently.

The silence stretched, and Lacy found her thoughts drifting, replaying the events of the day. The presentation, Mel's last-minute changes, the casual brush of Mel's hand against her shirt. She still felt the tingle where Mel's fingers had grazed her—completely accidental, but somehow it had left a mark.

Then there was the emotional hurt: the way Mel had overridden her adjustments to the deck, as if Lacy's input hadn't mattered.

She hadn't said anything yet, trying to tell herself it wasn't a big deal. But being stuck in a small space together was making all of her unspoken frustrations bubble to the surface.

"About the changes you made..." Lacy's voice was quiet, but it cut through the heavy silence.

Mel turned her head slightly, not fully meeting Lacy's eyes. "Let's talk about it later."

Lacy bristled. "Why not now?"

"Because—" Mel stopped herself, her mouth tightening into a thin line. *Because I'm too anxious to have a normal conversation.* "Because it's just politics, Lace. I had to."

Mel sighed, finally looking at her. "Look. I know you're new to this, but I promise it's not personal. It can happen – clients expect everything to be done yesterday. Sometimes that just means overriding our own decisions. Even good ones. And I'm still sorry I didn't tell you. But I wish you'd just...move on. "

The silence between them felt heavier now, filled with words that neither of them knew how to say. Lacy's thoughts raced, not just about the deck, but about everything. Working together had dredged up memories—things she hadn't planned on confronting now, or maybe ever. Moving on was the hardest thing she'd had to do when it came to Mel, and now...hearing Mel *tell* her to move on made everything feel worse.

She crossed her arms, her voice coming out shakier than she intended. "It's just...working together, it's brought up some...things I haven't thought about in a long time. I—don't know if I can handle being hurt like last time."

Mel's gaze flicked toward her, curious now, but still cautious. "Last time?"

Lacy bit her lip, unsure if she wanted to go down this road. But the words were already there, teetering on the edge, and there was no going back now. "You know...the way I used to feel about you."

Mel blinked, clearly startled. "Feel about me? What—how did you used to...?" She trailed off, as if she couldn't even say the words.

Lacy took a deep breath, her heart pounding in her chest. "I had a huge crush on you. Back in high school. I mean, I was practically in love with you." She let out a soft, bitter laugh. "I thought it was obvious, but...I guess it wasn't."

The confession hung in the air, sharp and painful, a wound being exposed for the first time.

Mel's face softened, her voice almost a whisper. "Lacy..."

"It didn't matter," Lacy said quickly, her words tumbling out in a rush. "Not after I saw you with Chet. I knew...it didn't matter how I felt. I was just some kid you tutored for extra credit."

Mel's eyes widened in shock. "Wait—you saw that?"

Lacy nodded, her throat tightening. "Yeah. So, I just...I let it go. Or I thought I did. But then you left for school, and I knew it was just...better I we didn't talk."

Mel's gaze was intense now, the tension between them shifting into something deeper, more complicated. "Lacy. I wish you had told me. Things might've been different."

Lacy turned to look at her, not sure if she should let herself hope. "How?"

Before Mel could answer, the elevator jolted slightly. They both froze, eyes flicking toward the door, just as it slid open with a soft chime.

They were at the lobby. A lobby filled with coworkers, and, unfortunately, Sophie happened to be waiting at the elevator doors.

"Ah, Mel, I was hoping to run into you—I had something I wanted to discuss for tomorrow, if you don't mind we walking you out?" She looked back and forth between the two women, pausing. "Unless there's something you need to handle here, in which case—"

The rush of reality was sudden, jarring. Lacy blinked, the weight of her confession still heavy on her chest, but there was no time, no space to process it. She stepped forward quickly, her cheeks burning, her mind spinning with everything she had just admitted. And in front of Sophie, who hopefully hadn't heard anything—*please, God, let her not have heard a word*—Lacy headed for the doors, with a quick, "No worries, see you tomorrow, goodnight," her heart pounding in her chest.

She didn't dare look back as she left the building, pretending not to hear Mel call her name.

Chapter 9: Confessions and Confusion

Mel pushed past Sophie, trying to follow Lacy from the building, but it was too late—by the time she got to the sidewalk, Lacy was long gone. Sophie followed Mel out of the building, the cool night air offering a brief reprieve from the stuffiness inside.

"What just happened there?" Sophie asked. It was clear Mel was anything but okay.

Mel stuffed her hands into her jacket pockets. "Honestly? I'm not sure."

Sophie gave a small nod, staying by her side as they walked slowly uptown. The city buzzed around them, cars honking, people milling about, and neon lights flickering in the distance. The chaotic energy felt far from what was swirling inside Mel's mind, a confusion she couldn't quite grasp.

As they neared the corner, Mel spotted a wine bar. The warm, low lighting felt inviting, a sharp contrast to the noise outside. Without thinking, she stopped short and turned to Sophie.

"Do you mind if we grab a drink?" Mel asked, half hoping Sophie would say yes, half expecting her to have plans.

Sophie glanced at the bar, then checked the time, then looked back at Mel, her expression softening. "Sounds like you could use it. To be honest, so could I. And, Mel—this conversation is off the record. I know we're getting to know each other, but I also can tell you need a friend right now, and while I won't cross professional boundaries—you clearly need someone to talk to. So. Let's talk."

They crossed the street and slipped into the bar, the atmosphere intimate but not crowded. It was one of those places that somehow made you feel both cozy and invisible at the same time. They found a small table near the back, and as they sat down, Mel felt the first real crack in her tension all day.

A waiter brought over menus, but Mel wasn't in the mood to browse. "Just a glass of Merlot, whatever you suggest," she said, waving off the menu. Sophie nodded and ordered the same.

Once the waiter was gone, Sophie leaned forward, her hands resting on the table. "So, what's going on? You've been on edge since we left the office. And whatever happened in that elevator did not look good."

Mel traced the rim of her glass with a finger, unsure where to begin. She thought about deflecting, saying it was nothing, but she knew Sophie could see right through that.

"Well, I just..." Mel began, her voice low. "It's about Lacy."

Sophie's eyebrows lifted slightly. "That was clear to everyone in the lobby."

Mel groaned. "Jeez. Yeah. Damn." The way she must have looked rushing after Lacy...how embarrassing. "Well. Anyway. You know I knew Lacy before this job...I told you some of the details, how I used to tutor her in high school. But after junior year, she just... stopped talking to me. I never knew why. I figured it wasn't a big deal. We weren't *that* close."

Sophie listened quietly, letting Mel get it out.

"And now, being around her, it's...it's bringing up feelings I didn't even know I had." Mel laughed, but it was humorless. "I didn't even realize back then that I could have had feelings for her. I wasn't out—not even to myself."

Sophie sipped her wine thoughtfully. "So, you've definitely got feelings for her now?"

"I think so," Mel admitted, feeling the words settle, the first time she'd ever said it out loud, but it felt *right*. "But that's not even the worst part. In the elevator tonight... Lacy told me she had a crush on me in high school. That's why she stopped talking to me—because she saw me kiss someone else. And I had no idea. It's like this whole thing has been sitting under the surface, and now it's... it's messing everything up."

Sophie set her glass down with a soft clink. "Wow. That's a lot."

"Yeah."

"And this other person... she's out of the picture?"

"He. I know, I don't even like men. I was—in denial. It was easier to just be straight and deal with my real feelings after I left school. Which was also after Lacy and I stopped talking." Mel ran a hand through her hair, frustration bubbling up. "And I don't even know what to do with that. I'm her boss now, there's the whole power dynamic. Plus, she still thinks I'm straight. I've never come out to her. Hell, I barely come out to myself half the time. Mostly because I barely ever date."

Sophie tilted her head, watching Mel with the steady gaze she always had, ever the perceptive one. "So, what do you want to do about it?"

Mel blinked, not expecting that question. "I don't know," she admitted. "I haven't dated anyone seriously in a long time. I'm not even sure I want to. But with Lacy...it's different. And I don't know how to navigate that, especially with work involved."

Sophie leaned back in her chair, crossing her arms thoughtfully. "It sounds like it might be wise to take Lacy off your team, or reassign you so you're not her direct supervisor. It'd eliminate the conflict of interest."

Mel frowned. "So, you definitely think I should tell her how I feel?"

Sophie shrugged. "I'm not saying you should rush anything. But if there's something there, you owe it to yourself—and to Lacy—to be honest. If there's more than just a teen crush there—well. Real love doesn't come around every day."

Mel chewed on that for a moment, rolling the idea around in her mind. Could she really put it all out there? Was it worth risking the rapport they'd begun to build professionally? And what if Lacy didn't feel the same way anymore?

"I just..." Mel started, then trailed off. "I don't want to screw things up for her. Or for me."

Sophie reached out, placing a hand on Mel's. "I understand. But you're already caught up in this thing. You've got to figure out what's more important—keeping the status quo or seeing if there's something there."

Mel nodded slowly, the weight of the decision settling in her chest. "Yeah," she murmured, more to herself than to Sophie.

"So," said Sophie, "On that note, I should get home before Blair starts wondering if I got lost on the way to the subway."

"The subway is five steps from the office."

Sophie smiled, and it was clear from the faraway look in her eyes that she wasn't thinking about Mel or their conversation, but about Blair, waiting at home for her. Their relationship sounded so...healthy. Loving. Something Mel had never really had.

"You two are lucky," Mel said.

"We are," said Sophie. "I don't know if what you have with Lacy is like what I have with Blair, but I just...I think you deserve happiness, Melissa. And I'm more than happy to pull some strings on my side. We won't fire Lacy—obviously—if that's a concern. But we can move her to another team, so you're not supervising her, and then the power dynamic won't be an issue."

Mel nodded, finishing her wine and paying for them both, in thanks for Sophie's advice. As they left the bar, Mel felt a little lighter, but confusion still buzzed at the edges of her mind.

As they parted ways at the subway entrance, Mel dug her phone out of her pocket. She had forgotten all about tomorrow—not a workday. A holiday.

Right, she thought, cursing herself for letting everything get so tangled up.

On impulse, she texted Lacy:

Hey, just a reminder that tomorrow's a holiday, so no need to come in. Hope you have a good night.

She stared at the message for a beat too long before hitting send. What was she even doing?

Mel shoved her phone back into her pocket and headed home, her mind circling the same dilemma. Feelings she'd denied for years had surfaced, and she had no idea what to do with them. The thought of telling Lacy how she felt was terrifying, but keeping it all inside might just be worse.

What she needed was a distraction. Mel pondered that as she loped down the subway steps. She hadn't been out in a while. Maybe she should see if her friend Bonnie was around—they always had fun together, and Bonnie had been a great wingwoman when they met at Prett. Mel loved having a hot straight girl with her when she went out—it nearly always meant other girls gravitated towards them, and Mel had gotten more than a few dates out of the situation. Bonnie was married, but her husband didn't mind if she wanted to go out, have some drinks, get hit on, and come home to him, as long as she was up front about her marital status (which she always was, in Mel's experience). Bonnie. A night out. That's exactly what she needed.

Chapter 10: Past Imperfect

A night out was exactly what she needed. After the events of the past few days, it was too much to stay at home and watch bad reality TV. So, Lacy adjusted her dress for what felt like the hundredth time in front of the mirror. Art had decided to stay one more night in the city, and it was he who suggested they spend that night going out on the town. After a night of Lacy weeping copiously into his shoulder why they watched *While You Were Sleeping*—a mutual favorite—she had agreed to give him a real night out somewhere fun before he went back home.

Besides, he'd argued, she needed a break after the week she'd had. And he was right. But was this dress too tight?

Art stuck his head around the bathroom door. "Damn! You *have* to wear that dress. And congratulations to me for picking it out for you, well done, good job, Art, you have excellent taste."

"Do you need me for this conversation, or are you good?" Lacy asked.

"I'm good," Art said, disappearing back around the corner. "Let me just get my shoes and I'll be ready to go."

In all honesty, the week had been *long*. Between the presentation, Mel's changes, and that moment in the elevator, Lacy couldn't seem to stop replaying everything in her head. That confession left her feeling exposed. She'd told Mel she'd had feelings for her in high school, and Mel hadn't run. In fact, she had seemed...softer. Curious. As if something shifted between them, but not in a bad way. Maybe Lacy wasn't the only one hiding her feelings? But Lacy had fled before the conversation could go anywhere deeper, and she just couldn't imagine Mel felt something for her—that stiff reminder not to come in to work today didn't exactly give Lacy hope for a blissful future together.

Now here she was, about to go out with Art, trying to push down the knot of anxiety in her chest. The look on Mel's face after the elevator doors had opened still haunted her mind.

"Time to go have fun," she muttered to herself, giving her reflection one last glance before grabbing her bag and heading out the door.

The club was loud, crowded, and, weirdly, just what Lacy needed to drown out the whirlwind in her brain. As soon as she stepped inside, bass thumped through her chest, and the lights flickered in rhythm to the music. Art was behind her, a big grin on his face.

"I'm getting us drinks. We need drinks!" he shouted over the music, putting an arm around her shoulder and guiding her to the bar.

Lacy smiled back, trying to get into the spirit of things. "Yes. Drinks. Multiple."

"First round's on me. Please let me order you something cheap so I can look like a nice friend, but not break the bank."

They pushed their way through throngs of people toward the bar. Lacy could feel the music pounding through her body, each beat pushing her to forget the events of the last few days. Art ordered her a cocktail, and she took a long sip, hoping the alcohol would do its job.

They settled near the dance floor, where the pulse of bodies moved like one entity. Art kept talking about his latest project—something about a startup, but Lacy wasn't really listening. She nodded, smiled in all the right places, but her mind was elsewhere. Specifically, it was on Mel.

"Earth to Lacy?" Art waved a hand in front of her face, jolting her back to the present. "You okay? You seem kind of out of it."

"I'm fine. Just... a lot on my mind."

Art raised an eyebrow but didn't push. "Well, I'm here to help you forget. Dance with me?"

Lacy hesitated, glancing around the room. The idea of dancing—of letting loose, letting go—was tempting. No. It was worth it. Tonight was all about her, and she *deserved* a fun night out, with hot go-go boys dancing on platforms near the bar, and watered down drinks, and way too much pop music she kind of hated but also kind of loved. It was what her brain needed to shut off, and she really needed her brain to shut off.

Lacy let Art lead her onto the dance floor, and let the music flow through her, finally allowing the tension of the week to release in a rush of movement and shared joy. She turned to Art, about to thank him for forcing her to go out tonight. This was such a wonderful idea!

But then she saw her.

Mel.

Her breath caught in her throat, and her heart seemed to stop completely. There, across the room, was Mel—leaning against the side of the bar they'd just vacated, her hand on the arm of a blonde woman Lacy didn't recognize. They seemed to be talking to a third woman. Then, without hesitation, Mel leaned in and kissed the blonde.

It was like a punch to the gut.

Lacy's mind went blank. She couldn't think, couldn't breathe. The sight of Mel once again pressed against someone else felt like someone had yanked the rug from under her. She couldn't move, couldn't tear her eyes away from the scene before her.

Art, noticing her sudden shift, followed her gaze. "Wait, is that...?"

Lacy swallowed hard. "Yeah," she whispered, the word inaudible over the music. "That's Mel."

Before Art could say anything, Lacy turned on her heel and pushed her way toward the exit. She needed air. She needed to *not* be there. This had been a terrible idea.

The cold night air hit her like a slap in the face as she stumbled out onto the sidewalk. The pounding in her chest had nothing to do with the music this time. She felt stupid. So, so stupid. All that time worrying about how Mel might react to her confession, and here she was, making out with someone else. With a *woman*. Was Mel gay? Bi? Pan? God, did it even matter? She clearly wasn't interested in Lacy, and that was really the only important question in any context.

I guess that probably was her at the bar during college, Lacy thought. *I guess maybe this isn't the first time she's kissed a woman. How could I have missed that?*

She didn't know why she thought things might be different. Maybe because of the way Mel had looked at her in the elevator, or how she'd seemed to change after Lacy had admitted her feelings. But it didn't matter now, did it? Mel was clearly fine, and with someone else. Again. The hurt that she felt in high school compounded, and Lacy realized, suddenly, that there were tears running down her cheeks.

"God," she said under her breath, pulling out her phone and searching for an Uber. "I gotta get out of here."

"Lacy!"

The sound of Mel's voice jolted her out of her thoughts. She whirled around, seeing Mel running out of the club and toward her, breathless and confused.

"Lacy, wait!"

"Why?" Lacy snapped, her emotions bubbling over. "So you can explain why you're kissing random women like none of this ever happened?"

Mel froze, clearly caught off guard. "What are you talking about?"

"That kiss," Lacy spat, pointing back toward the club. "You—" She broke off, her chest tightening as she struggled to find the right words. "You kissed someone else. After everything, after—"

"After what?" Mel's voice was louder now, and there was something raw in it, something Lacy wasn't prepared for. "What are you really upset about, Lacy? You told me you *had* a crush on me in high school, past tense, as if it wasn't a thing anymore. What's really going on here?"

Lacy's throat tightened. She felt the anger rising, but beneath it, there was hurt. So much hurt she didn't know how to contain it anymore.

"I don't know," she admitted finally, her voice breaking. "But you know what, it doesn't matter. I just—I'm always going after impossible things, I guess. And I was wrong. Again. That's on me."

For a moment, Mel just stared at her, and Lacy felt like the world was tilting. Then, without warning, Mel stepped forward, grabbing her arm—not hard, but enough to stop her from leaving.

"You weren't wrong," Mel said quietly, her voice barely a whisper. "Not about how I feel."

Before Lacy could react, Mel leaned in, her lips brushing against Lacy's in a kiss that was both desperate and tender. It was nothing like the kiss Lacy had seen back in the club, which had looked...a little awkward, to be honest. But this—this felt like the culmination of everything that had been building between them: tension, confusion, unspoken words.

When they finally pulled apart, Lacy's heart was racing, her mind spinning. She was about to pull Mel back, needing to taste her lips again, when Mel started to say something—

"I—" Mel began, but the words seemed to die in her throat.

Lacy looked into Mel's eyes, seeing confusion, panic—and that made the decision for her. This had been a terrible idea. Mel didn't want this. She was just humoring Lacy. She probably wanted that other woman all along—who had just come out of the bar behind them, clearly looking for Mel. Lacy didn't wait for an explanation. She turned, climbing into her Uber and leaving Mel on the sidewalk.

She was scared, she admitted to herself, but still—that had been a terrible idea. Because what just happened...was something neither of them could take back.

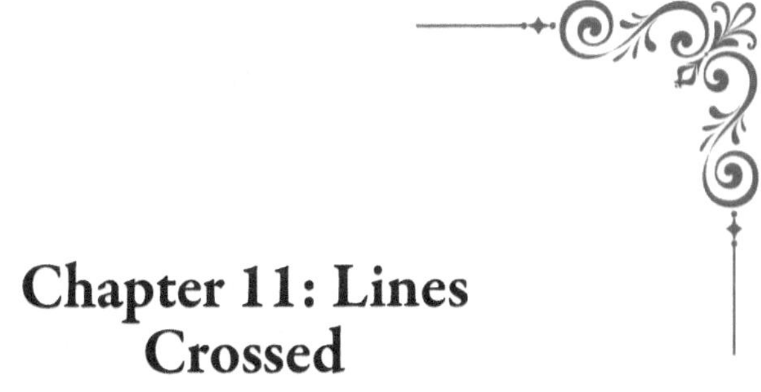

Chapter 11: Lines Crossed

Mel woke to the blaring of her alarm, but the noise did little to rouse her from the tangled mess of thoughts that had plagued her since last night. She had tossed and turned for hours, replaying every moment of the confrontation with Lacy on the sidewalk outside the club.

Her head throbbed. Groping for her phone, she saw the time. It seemed like it was too early to be up on a day off, which she'd been smart enough to schedule after Bonnie agreed to go out with her last night. But she knew she had set that alarm for a reason—otherwise, she'd be liable to sleep till noon. She'd texted and called Lacy last night, multiple times, but had gotten no response. Eventually, the phone just went straight to voicemail.

But that kiss she'd shared with Lacy was vivid in her mind, a splash of color against a canvas of confusion. *Ugh. And she was such a good kisser*, Mel remembered. *Goddammit.* She hauled herself out of bed and making her way to the kitchen.

She brewed a pot of coffee. As she waited for the caffeine to kick in, she sank into a chair in her living room, her thoughts swirling. The single question in her mind was simple: How had things gotten so complicated?

Her phone buzzed, and she glanced at the screen to see a notification from a dating podcast she occasionally listened to. The episode's title, "Navigating Complicated Feelings: Live Episode," caught her eye. Maybe it was a sign. Mel laughed. She didn't believe in signs. Still, she tapped on the notification and began to listen, hoping for some semblance of clarity.

The podcast's hosts discussed relationship dilemmas, offering advice on how to handle emotions, confrontations, and misunderstandings. Mel found herself hanging on every word, particularly when the conversation turned to unresolved feelings and the importance of communication.

One host, a soothing voice full of empathy, said, "When you've crossed lines and things are left unresolved, it's crucial to address them. Avoiding the situation only compounds confusion and hurts more in the long run."

Mel nodded along. *Yes. Exactly. Do something.* She had to fix whatever mess she had inadvertently created. The thought of letting Lacy slip away, leaving things so unfinished, was making her miserable.

She picked up her phone and found the podcast's call-in number, fingers trembling slightly. After a few rings, a cheerful voice greeted her.

"Hi, you're live on 'Love & Life,' talking alllllll about complicated feelings—how can we help you today?"

Mel took a deep breath, trying to steady her nerves. "Hi, my name is Mel—inda," she panicked, realizing she'd still said a name slightly too close to her own. *But, fuck it, in for a penny, right?* "I have a complicated situation with someone, and I'm not sure how to approach it. I think I crossed some lines, and I'm worried if I don't address it, everything will get worse."

There was a brief pause as the host took in her words. "It sounds like you're in a tough spot. What's the main issue you're facing?"

"I...I kissed someone I work with. Someone I've known for a while. And she ran away. And I tried texting and calling, but she hasn't answered. I'm not sure if we should try to fix it, or if I should just pretend nothing happened or if there's some other fix I haven't come up with."

The host's voice was calm. "It's understandable to feel conflicted. And I don't know your work policy, so just be aware that this is not legal advice, and if you get in trouble, I'm not liable for anything, got it?"

Mel laughed, "Yeah, I got it."

"So, the key is to address your feelings directly with the other person. Avoiding the situation will make things more complicated. Don't ask how I know that." She paused for the co-host's inevitable laughter. "If you're serious about resolving things, it's important to have an honest conversation. Tell her what you want. See how she feels. If she's not into it, back off. If she is into it, then you have something else to figure out."

Mel listened carefully. "You're right. That's really helpful." *And I guess I could've gotten the same advice from a fortune cookie, but it's still good advice.*

"Good luck, Melinda. And remember, clarity and communication are key."

After ending the call, Mel sat in silence. Despite its mundane response, the podcast had given her the push she needed. She had to talk to Lacy. But how would she, when Lacy wasn't answering her messages? Was it okay to try to see her in person, or was that tantamount to stalking? She didn't want to be some psycho, and she didn't want to invade Lacy's privacy. But she'd seen hurt in Lacy's eyes last night, and she had to know if she could fix it.

Mel gathered her phone, keys, wallet. She needed to at least try to talk about things before they spiraled further.

As she approached Lacy's apartment building, Mel felt a knot of anxiety in her stomach. She took a deep breath and rolled her shoulders back a couple times. *Be cool, Mel,* before ringing the doorbell.

Lacy opened the door, her face both surprise and apprehension. "What are you doing here?"

"You didn't answer my calls or texts, and if you want me to go, I will, but I just wanted to see if we could talk," Mel said, her voice firm but tinged with hesitance.

Lacy glanced back into the apartment, and Mel worried that she might have someone there. *God, what if she's got a girl in there, and I just ruined her morning.*

"My phone died," Lacy said, "In the Uber. I plugged it in, but I must have forgotten to turn it on. That's my fault." But she didn't step back to let Mel in, and Mel thought that was probably a sign for her to go.

"Oh," she said. "Well. I hope you get that figured out, I guess." She turned around, but this time it was Lacy who reached out and put a hand on her arm.

"Wait," she said. "Come in. We'll talk."

Lacy's apartment was small but cozy, a stark contrast to the tension that filled the space between them. There were some beer bottles on the table. Lacy swiped them up and took them to the trash. "Art," she said. "He left this morning. And isn't much on cleaning up."

Mel took a seat on the couch, and Lacy finished a quick tidy, then sat next to her, keeping a full cushion's distance apart.

"I didn't come here to make things awkward," Mel struggled to find the words. "I just wanted to clear the air. I feel like I overstepped, and I'm sorry."

Lacy's gaze was steady, but there was a hint of something else. *Could it be desire? Please let her still want me.* After that kiss, Mel wanted nothing more than to kiss Lacy again. But she held back.

"Look, Mel, I appreciate that you're trying to—make this right. But I need to be honest. This is a lot for me. I just feel like we should keep our distance from each other."

Mel's heart sank. "Why? I thought maybe—"

"No," Lacy interrupted, shaking her head. "It's not just about...the kiss. It's everything. I had hoped things could be different, but I don't want to risk getting hurt again. It took me years to get over—and then to see you with that woman—brought things up all over again. We should just stay—work colleagues, I guess. It's better that way."

Mel felt a wave of regret wash over her. "Years—? Lace, I—please, don't interrupt, let me work this out."

Lacy sat there, letting Mel think it through.

"You saw me at the club kissing Bonnie. And that's why you ran out of there."

Lacy nodded, letting Mel continue.

"Bonnie's an old friend. This is going to sound ludicrous—it sounds ludicrous to me, even as I'm saying it—but she's straight. We had a bet going that some awful woman had told her that if she just kissed the right woman she'd turn gay, and I happened to be there, and Bonnie trusts me and knows I would never do anything—anyway, she asked if I'd kiss her to prove the other woman wrong, and if we won, she'd give us fifty bucks. Which, by the way, we did win. So. Bonnie's straight. I can't say she's the first straight woman I've kissed, though I haven't ever been paid for it before."

Lacy's eyes had changed as Mel went through the story, from guarded to amused.

"Somebody really made that bet?"

Mel pulled out her phone, "I'll prove it."

She called Bonnie, putting her on speaker.

"What up biotch?" Bonnie answered.

"Well, it's the 21st century, so you should probably stop answering the phone that way," Mel said.

"Yeah, yeah. You never call. What's this about? Do you miss me? Oooh, did our kiss turn you straight?"

Mel grimaced. "I was just wondering—I'm here with my friend Lacy, and—"

"Lacy. The hot one?"

"—and you're on speaker," Mel finished, way too late.

Lacy had turned beet red, but was laughing.

"Hi, Bonnie," she choked out, "I think I might like you."

"Well, I am a gay chick magnet. Sorry if you're not gay, I shouldn't have assumed," Bonnie replied.

"Nope, you got it right. Totally gay," said Lacy.

"Another win for me." Bonnie laughed. "So, what do you need?"

"Would you mind telling Lacy what happened last night at the club?" Mel left it open-ended, not wanting to seem like she was swaying Bonnie at all.

"Oh, yeah, no problem. This chick Norma comes over—which, what an old-timey name, no?—and she wants me to dance or to buy me a drink, and I'm like no, I'm here to get my friend laid, not myself, thank you, and I don't even like girls, and Norma is like, yeah, right, I can change you, and I'm like no, that's not how it works, so anyway it comes down to Norma thinking if I just kiss the right girl I'll be all into girls, so I tell her 'Norma, honey, the only girl for me is my friend Mel, who I've known since college, and we have not hooked up, but I can tell that she would be an amazing lover'—sorry if that's TMI, Mel, but I did say that—'and anyway, if anyone was gonna turn me, it'd be her.' So then we kissed, and it did nothing for me, and Norma gave me fifty bucks and walked away."

Lacy sat back on the couch.

"Thanks, Bonnie," said Mel. "I'll call you later."

She turned to Lacy, waiting for her to say something.

"I'm sorry I made an assumption last night. That wasn't fair to you. And Bonnie seems nice."

"She is," said Mel, worried about the tone of Lacy's words.

"I just need some time to think," said Lacy. "Just...give me some space, okay?"

Mel nodded, hope dying. She wanted to argue, to convince Lacy that things could be different, but she knew Lacy wasn't one to change her mind easily.

"Okay," Mel said quietly, standing up. "I understand. Thank you for being honest with me."

Lacy stood as well. "Goodbye, Mel."

Mel nodded, her heart heavy as she left the apartment. The door closed behind her with a quiet thud, and she walked away feeling like she had failed, somehow—crossed lines that could never be uncrossed. Even the truth didn't sway Lacy. She'd never have a chance at a relationship with her. She'd have to find a way to get over it.

All she could do now was try to find her own way forward, even if it meant letting go of something that had barely begun.

Chapter 12: Breaking Point

Sophie had expected the day to be challenging, but the morning had surpassed her expectations.

As Sophie prepared for a client presentation, she sensed the air thick with unspoken tension. She had hoped that the meeting would serve as neutral ground, where both Mel and Lacy could demonstrate their professionalism. Instead, it became a battleground.

The meeting room was buzzing with the usual pre-presentation chatter. Mel, at the head of the table, was reviewing her notes with precision. Lacy, two seats away from her, was shuffling through papers and occasionally glancing at Mel, her expression showing both apprehension and determination.

The client, a stern-looking man in his early fifties, sat at the end of the table, seemingly unimpressed by pre-meeting pleasantries. Mel began her presentation, but the tension between her and Lacy was palpable. Their professional masks barely concealed the underlying discord.

Mel clicked through the slides, her voice steady, but edged with frustration. "As you can see, our proposal outlines a comprehensive strategy that will leverage our strengths and address key pain points."

Lacy's hand shot up. "Actually, we discussed adding more detail to the budget projections. The numbers here don't reflect what we agreed upon."

Mel's eyes narrowed. "Lacy, we finalized this last week. I'm not sure why there's a discrepancy."

The client shifted in his seat, clearly uncomfortable with the unfolding argument. "Is this part of the presentation, or do you want to finish this conversation privately?"

Mel, her face flushed with frustration, tried to maintain her composure. "Don't worry. Everything's fine."

Lacy's tone grew sharper. "But these figures are important. If we don't correct them, we're not presenting an accurate picture."

The argument escalated, voices rising. Sophie, who had been observing from the sidelines, intervened. "Ladies. We're here to present a proposal, not to argue. If there are specifics that need to be adjusted, we can go over those afterwards."

Both women fell silent, though their expressions were far from reconciled. Sophie's intervention did little to diffuse the tension; if anything, it highlighted the depth of their discord.

After the meeting, Sophie pulled Mel and Lacy aside. "We need to address what happened in there. This kind of behavior is unacceptable. I'll need to speak with both of you individually."

Mel, anxiety palpable, nodded. "I understand."

As Mel walked back to her office, she felt a heavy weight on her shoulders. She had hoped the day would be a turning point, but instead, it seemed to have exposed the rift between her and Lacy. She knew she had made mistakes, but Lacy's actions were contributing to a deeper problem.

Mel's heart sank when she saw Lacy packing at her desk. Panic gripped her as she wondered if Lacy was being fired. The sight of Lacy methodically placing her personal items into a box made Mel's stomach churn.

Sophie watched from her office door, her expression a mix of sympathy and resolution. She had hoped that transferring Lacy to a department on another floor—so the two of them wouldn't need to interact at all—would help alleviate the strain from this morning's events. It was the last solution she could come up with.

Mel went into her own office and sank into her seat. She prided herself on her professionalism, but today had been a stark reminder that even the most well-laid plans could unravel.

Mel's phone buzzed with a notification: a message from Sophie, informing the office that Lacy had transferred to a different team three floors away. Mel read the message with a sinking feeling, knowing that this was not the end but rather the beginning of a new chapter in her relationship with Lacy.

Sophie's decision to move Lacy was intended to provide both women with the space they needed to process their emotions and move forward. It was a difficult but necessary step to ensure a more harmonious work environment.

As Mel sat alone in her office, she couldn't help but replay the day's events in her mind. She had hoped for a resolution, but instead, she felt as though she had been thrust into a complex web of misunderstandings. She needed to find a way to make things right.

Mel's thoughts were interrupted by a knock on her office door. It was Sophie. "I would have waited for you to come by my office, but it seemed like I might be waiting all day," Sophie said, with a hint of amusement.

Mel forced a smile. "I'm sorry. I'm just... processing."

Sophie nodded, expression thoughtful. "I know this has been a tough day. I want you to know that you're not alone. We'll figure things out."

"So...neither of us is fired?" Mel clarified.

Sophie shook her head. "A stricter boss would have you both out on the street, but you've given me enough background to know that separating the two of you is probably the best solution here. You're both excellent at your jobs, and when you're not fighting, you do work well together. We would be hard pressed to replace you both at the same time. Just...give it a few days, take some time apart. If you want to take some vacation days, you have PTO. Just do whatever you need to clear your head and get back in the game."

Mel appreciated the gesture but couldn't shake a feeling of helplessness.

"Thanks, Sophie. I think, actually, I might take the rest of the day off."

"I think that's a wise idea," Sophie replied.

As Mel gathered her things and left the office, she couldn't help but think about Lacy and the unresolved tension.

Sophie saw Mel's defeated expression as she exited the building. She knew Mel was struggling, but she also felt she had made the right decision in moving Lacy. It was a difficult choice, but it was one that Sophie hoped would ultimately benefit both women. She felt bad that Lacy kept getting shuffled around, as if she was replaceable; it was clear the young woman had talent and determination, and though the setting wasn't appropriate, her pushback against Mel on the numbers had somewhat impressed Sophie. She needed people who cared about the work they did, and who were willing to challenge something if it wasn't correct. But not in the middle of client presentations.

And, moreover, she worried about how this would all impact both Mel and Lacy, and if they would be able to put aside their differences. They were at their best when they could collaborate, and she still held out hope that the two of them would be able to work cross-functionally, in some way.

As Mel left the office, she knew that she needed to find a way to make amends, but the road ahead seemed fraught with obstacles. For now, all she could do was hope that time would bring clarity and resolution.

Chapter 13: Silent Treatment

The office was quieter than usual when Mel arrived the next morning. The usual hum of activity was replaced by a subdued atmosphere that seemed to echo the tension of the previous day. Mel was still reeling from the events of the day before, trying to make sense of everything that had happened. The fact that Lacy had been moved to another department was a blow Mel hadn't anticipated. She realized she wouldn't even see Lacy most days, which was rather upsetting.

Mel's footsteps echoed through the corridor as she walked to her office. The sight of Lacy's now-empty desk left a lingering ache in her heart.

As she began her workday, Mel tried to focus on her tasks. However, her mind kept drifting. She glanced at the clock, noting the time. She hadn't seen Lacy since yesterday, and neither one of them had texted or emailed the other. The silence was deafening.

Mel's phone buzzed with a message from Sophie, reminding her of a meeting later in the day. Mel responded absently. This was going to be a long day. The morning passed slowly, with Mel's mind wandering between her work and her lingering feelings. She found herself growing anxious, wondering if Lacy was intentionally avoiding coming up to their floor, or if she was preoccupied with her new role.

During lunch, Mel decided to grab a quick bite from the café downstairs. As she entered the small space, she scanned the room for any sign of Lacy, who she knew sometimes grabbed lunch down here. The café was bustling, but no Lacy. Mel's heart sank.

When Mel returned to the office, she was surprised to see Lacy walking briskly down the hall. Lacy's demeanor was notably different—she was completely absorbed in work, not looking at her phone or anything else. The dreamer who had been so often lost in thought now seemed gone. Mel felt a pang of hurt as she watched Lacy move with purpose, feeling like an outsider to the world Lacy was now a part of. She was about to try to catch up to her, when Lacy turned the corner and walked down the stairs, and then it was too late to follow her without looking like a stalker.

As the afternoon wore on, Mel's frustration grew. She tried to focus on work, but the nagging concern about Lacy's assignment and their unresolved issues kept intruding.

By the time the workday was nearing its end, Mel's patience wore thin. She decided to take a chance and find Lacy downstairs in the kitchen, where she knew they would have a moment of privacy. Lacy always grabbed coffee between 4:00 and 4:30, and while it felt awkward to rush downstairs in the hopes of catching her, Mel knew they needed to talk after that meeting debacle.

As Mel walked into the kitchen, she found Lacy grabbing a soda from the fridge. *God, she isn't even drinking her usual coffee anymore,* Mel thought. She took a deep breath and approached Lacy, her heart pounding.

"Can we talk?" Mel asked, her voice hesitant.

Lacy looked up, her expression entirely blank. "What's up?"

Mel took a moment to gather her thoughts. "I know you've been moved to another department. Obviously. On another floor. I mean, also obviously. I didn't ask Sophie to move you. I just wanted to see if everything is okay."

Lacy's eyes remained distant. "I'm fine. I'm just on a different team. It's not a big deal."

Mel's heart sank at Lacy's nonchalant response. "I just wanted to make sure you were alright."

Lacy's gaze dropped to the floor, her voice barely above a whisper. "It's just...complicated. I needed a change. Things were getting too awkward, and after talking with Sophie, it seemed like the best solution."

Mel felt a knot form in her stomach. She thought Sophie had made the decision, but to hear that Lacy had asked for a transfer to get away from her just made things worse. "I want you to know I'm sorry about how I acted in the meeting. I should have given you more space to explain."

Lacy looked up, her eyes filled with a mixture of sadness and resignation. "Look. That was on me. I overstepped there. But, Mel, it's not about work. It's about everything. I can't keep getting my heart broken."

Mel's heart ached at Lacy's words. "I get it. If there's a chance for me to make things right, I'd like to try. I—I feel things for you, too, Lace."

Lacy shook her head. "You just—don't feel the way I do. And that's okay, you don't have to. But I need to move on and find someone who does."

Before Mel could respond, Lacy turned and walked out of the kitchen, leaving Mel standing alone with her thoughts. The emptiness of the room mirrored the emptiness Mel felt inside. *Why won't she give us a chance?* Mel wanted to know. *I do have feelings for her. Real feelings.*

She took a moment, leaning against the sink. *I guess if I had seen her making out someone right when I thought we might be able to have something real happen between us, I would have been pretty devastated.* And, Mel realized, it must have reminded Lacy of what happened in high school with Chet. God, she had terrible luck with Lacy.

Mel walked to her office, her mind a whirlwind of emotions. She closed the door behind her and slumped into her chair, feeling a deep sense of disappointment. She had hoped for resolution, but instead, she felt like she had reached an impasse.

Sophie watched as Mel retreated to her office, her expression defeated. She knew that moving Lacy to another department was a difficult decision, but it was one that Sophie hoped would ultimately be beneficial. The tension between Mel and Lacy had been palpable, and it was clear that their interactions had become too argumentative to continue working together effectively.

The evening was quiet as Mel made her way home. Her thoughts were a jumble of confusion and regret, and she couldn't shake the feeling that things had gone horribly wrong. She needed to find a way to address the situation with Lacy, but the path forward seemed entirely blocked off.

Chapter 14: Reevaluating the Brief

Mel sat alone at her desk. Her workspace was cluttered with notes, drafts, and endless revisions. The new assistant, Karen, despite her eagerness, was proving inadequate. Her lack of familiarity with the project made the already challenging task even more difficult.

Mel glanced at the clock and sighed heavily. The presentation was later that afternoon, and time was slipping away. This client was demanding, with high stakes and more expectations. Every detail needed to be flawless. The pressure felt like a vice squeezing around her, and Mel's nerves were fraying.

Karen sat studiously at her desk, diligent but inexperienced. Mel's frustration grew as she constantly corrected errors. It was clear that Karen's assistance, while well-meaning, was falling short of what was needed. And though Mel had tutored difficult people in the past, she didn't have time to teach someone the ins and outs of the ad world.

By mid-afternoon, Mel was on the verge of breaking down. The presentation, intended to be a collaborative effort, had turned into a solo endeavor. Mel's focus, once sharp and clear, had become a chaotic mess of revisions.

Mel knew she needed to speak with Sophie. There was no way she could pull this off without more help. She dreaded asking for help, but there was no way around it.

Mel made her way to Sophie's office, her thoughts racing with worries about the presentation and her own performance. As she entered, Sophie looked up from her desk, which she somehow always managed to keep organized. Mel's desk in recent days had become a chaotic mess.

"Have a seat," Sophie said, indicating the chair opposite her. "What's going on?"

Mel took a seat, feeling the weight of her anxiety. "I'm really struggling with this presentation. Karen—the new assistant—she's trying, but she's not getting it. I keep thinking about how well Lacy and I worked together."

Sophie's eyebrows arched slightly. "You're asking if Lacy can assist you with the presentation?"

"I know it's a lot to ask, but Lacy understands the project. She knows what the client's going for. I really need her expertise right now."

Sophie leaned back in her chair, her gaze thoughtful. "You're aware that reassigning Lacy was a significant decision. She's in a different department for a reason."

Mel nodded, her eyes pleading. "I get that. But this is a crucial presentation. I promise it's a one-time request. I just need her help to get it right."

Sophie studied Mel's face, assessing the sincerity in her eyes. "Alright. I'll speak with Lacy and see if she's willing to help you. But you need to handle this professionally."

"I promise," Mel said earnestly. "I just need her help today. After that, back to no contact."

Sophie squinted at that, about to comment, but holding back. "I'll see what I can do," she said, typing quickly on her computer.

Mel returned to her desk and anxiously awaited a response. Time seemed to crawl. Finally, Lacy entered the office, carrying her laptop.

"Hi," Lacy said, her tone neutral.

"Hi," Mel replied, a mixture of relieved and apprehensive. "Thanks for coming."

Lacy remained standing, despite the open chair across from Mel's desk. "Sophie mentioned you needed help with the presentation."

Mel took a deep breath. *Focus on business.* "This client has specific needs, and I'm worried we're not going to meet their expectations."

Lacy nodded, her expression softening. "Show me what you have. I'll see where we can make improvements. We'll get it ready."

For the next few hours, Mel and Lacy worked side by side, meticulously reviewing each slide. Lacy's insight proved invaluable, and Mel felt a renewed sense of hope as the clock ticked closer to the presentation time. She glanced at her watch and realized they had less than an hour before they needed to be in the conference room. The pressure was intense, but having Lacy's help made a difference.

When the presentation was finally complete, Mel knew it was a solid piece of work. Still, her personal anxiety lingered. *But not about the presentation*, she knew, being honest with herself. *I'm bothered by how much I like having her next to me. I'm bothered by the fact that she looks so good today. I'm bothered by so many things that have nothing to do with work, and I can't do anything about any of it, because I'm a coward.*

She groaned, and Lacy looked at her quizzically. "What's wrong?"

"Nothing," Mel replied, too quickly. "Just tired. This is great," she motioned to the presentation. "I really couldn't have done this without you."

Lacy's eyes narrowed, not buying Mel's excuse. "I'm glad I could help. But, Mel, I wanted to say—"

Just as she was about to finish the statement, there was a knock on the door. Karen poked her head in. "The client is here."

Lacy stood up, preparing to leave. "Great. You've got this."

Mel wanted to know what Lacy was going to ask. She wanted to call her to come back, tell Karen to get her face out of there, but it was too late to do anything, and she let Lacy leave, feeling a pang of sadness. Despite their collaboration, the personal distance between them remained.

Mel headed to the conference room. She was always nervous before presentations, even when she was prepared. She breathed deeply, forced herself to stay calm. The client was already seated. As Mel walked into the conference room, her eyes flicked to the side. Through the glass walls of the room, she saw Lacy passing. Lacy's head was down, checking her phone, a small smile on her face, and she didn't look up to meet Mel's gaze. Mel's heart sank at the sight. *Who is she texting? Is she seeing someone? She would have told me, right? But—no, not the time to dwell on this.* She swallowed hard, pushing back the pain. Her emotions were all over the place, but she had a job to finish.

Mel plastered on a professional smile. As she began the presentation, she took one last look at Lacy through the glass window. The sight of her walking away without a backward glance was like a physical blow. *Fix this*, Mel thought to herself. *Whatever it takes. Fix this.*

Chapter 15: Mixed Messages

Lacy sat at her desk, the remnants of the client presentation still visible on her screen. Despite the late hour, the office was unusually quiet. Most of her colleagues had already left, leaving Lacy alone with her thoughts and the unresolved tension that seemed to cling to the air. The frustration she felt was gnawing at her, leaving her restless and on edge.

She had spent the entire day grappling with the realization that, despite everything, she was being pulled back into the orbit of Mel's professional world. It wasn't just that Mel had asked for her help; it was the confusion that came with it. On one hand, she had been told—implicitly if not explicitly—that working closely with Mel was off-limits due to their complicated history. On the other hand, Mel's actions had said otherwise, blurring the lines between their personal issues and their professional responsibilities.

Lacy's phone buzzed on her desk, pulling her from her thoughts. It was Art. She picked it up and answered with a distracted, "Hey."

"Hey, Lacy. How's it going?" Art's voice was warm and reassuring, a stark contrast to Lacy's internal turmoil.

"I'm fine. Just dealing with some mixed signals from work," Lacy replied, her tone reflecting her frustration. "Mel's been acting all professional and distant, but then she pulls me into this project, and I don't even know what to make of it."

Art's voice turned concerned. "That sounds rough. What's the project about?"

"It's the new client presentation," Lacy said, running a hand through her hair. "She needed my help last minute to fix some slides. It feels like... like she's trying to walk a tightrope between keeping things professional and dragging me back into this mess."

"Is this making you reconsider staying at the company?" Art asked, a hint of unease in his voice.

"Honestly, I'm not sure," Lacy admitted. "I mean, I started out here wanting to prove myself and make a mark. But if it's just going to be this kind of emotional and professional rollercoaster, I don't know if it's worth it."

Art sighed softly. "Sometimes it's hard to see the bigger picture when you're caught up in the middle of it all. Maybe you need to take a step back and think about what you really want."

"Yeah," Lacy said. "I think I need some time to figure that out. I'm supposed to catch up with Mel about the project tomorrow, but right now, all I want to do is get some distance from this place."

"Well, if you need to talk more, you know where to find me," Art said. "Take care of yourself, okay?"

"Thanks, Art. I will," Lacy replied, hanging up the call. She took a deep breath and tried to calm her racing thoughts.

As she gathered her things, her mind drifted back to the presentation she had helped with. The whole situation felt like déjà vu—being used for her skills while being kept at arm's length emotionally. It was a reminder of how things had been in her early days at the job, when she was still trying to find her footing and make a name for herself.

Lacy's frustration was compounded by her growing sense of being caught in a cycle of mixed messages. Mel's professional demeanor suggested that everything was business as usual, but the fact that she had reached out to Lacy for help hinted at unresolved feelings and complexities. It was as though Mel was trying to navigate a maze of her own making, dragging Lacy along in the process.

Lacy was just about to leave when she received an email notification. It was from Sophie, with a subject line that caught her attention: "Feedback on Presentation." Lacy hesitated before opening it, bracing herself for more of the same mixed signals. She skimmed through the email and felt her frustration shift to surprise. The client had been impressed with the presentation. They were requesting Lacy to be involved in their next project, alongside Mel.

The realization hit her like a ton of bricks. She had been so caught up in her own frustrations that she hadn't considered how well the project had actually gone. And now, she was facing the prospect of being pulled back into the very world she was trying to distance herself from. The client's request felt like a double-edged sword—a chance to prove herself again but also a reminder of the emotional mess she was entangled in.

Lacy's mind raced as she considered her options. Should she accept the client's request and work with Mel again, or should she walk away and avoid further complications? She didn't have an answer yet, but she knew she would need to decide soon.

As she walked out of the office, Lacy's thoughts were consumed by the prospect of working with Mel again. The mixed messages and emotional turmoil she had experienced made her question whether she was willing to subject herself to another round of heartache and confusion. The decision loomed large in her mind, and she knew that she would need to weigh her options carefully.

Lacy took a deep breath, trying to steady her nerves. The path ahead was uncertain, and the mixed signals she was receiving only added to her sense of frustration and confusion. She would need to confront her feelings and make a choice, but for now, all she could do was navigate the maze of emotions and decisions that lay before her.

Chapter 16: Aftermath

Mel was alone in her apartment, surrounded by the familiar clutter of books and old magazines, but today it felt oppressive, rather than comforting. The afternoon sun cast a warm glow through the blinds, but it did little to alleviate the chill of Mel's isolation. She had taken the day off from work, a decision that had seemed prudent the night before but now felt like a poor choice. She stared at the half-empty bottle of wine on the coffee table, contemplating another glass but feeling the heaviness of the decision.

The doorbell rang, jolting her from her thoughts. Mel groaned, barely mustering the energy to rise. She shuffled to the door, opening it to find Lacy standing there with a paper bag from Mel's favorite takeout place. Lacy's presence was unexpected and disarming.

"Hey," Lacy said, offering a tentative smile. "I heard you were off today and thought you might want some lunch."

Mel blinked, surprised. "Lacy? What are you doing here?"

"I brought you chicken fried rice," Lacy said, holding up the bag. "I don't actually know if you still even like chicken fried rice, but I figured you might need something to eat, and if you don't like chicken fried rice, I can eat it or we can find someone in the office who might want it—"

"Stop," said Mel, her mind still clouded by the wine. "You've said chicken fried rice too many times, but it is kind of adorable that you remember I used to like that as a kid. And still do like it as an adult. So.

Yes. Please. Come in where there is a table to sit at and eat things like a human."

She led Lacy into the living room, which was a mess of discarded tissues and empty wine glasses. The sight of the clutter made Mel's heart sink.

"I...might have overestimated the human part of things. Sorry," Mel said, quickly grabbing a small trash bin and gathering up tissues. Lacy picked up the wine glasses and brought them to the kitchen sink, rinsing them out.

"You don't have to do my dishes," Mel said from the other room, still tidying.

"I'm not," said Lacy, "But I am going to want an explanation for this, and I'm not leaving till we talk it out." Lacy returned to the living room where the bag of food sat on the coffee table and began unpacking it, revealing the familiar containers. "I honestly didn't know if you'd be up for talking, but I thought at least you might want some food."

Mel watched her, a twinge of gratitude mingling with guilt. "You didn't have to come all this way."

Lacy looked up. "I wanted to. I know things are complicated right now. But I'm still here, at least. Okay?"

Mel felt a lump in her throat, emotions bubbling to the surface. "Thank you," she said quietly. "I really appreciate it."

They settled on the couch, and Mel took a tentative bite of the chicken fried rice. The taste was comforting, a small reminder of better times. Lacy watched her eat, a hint of a smile playing on her lips. After a few moments, Mel set her fork down and sighed deeply.

"Lacy, I owe you an apology," Mel began, her voice heavy with regret. "I didn't handle things well in that meeting. I was a mess. And I get that you probably feel bad about seeing me with Bonnie, but I promise, it was really not a thing."

Lacy shook her head. "It's not just about that. Our past—it still hurts. And I get that you say you want to give us a shot, but then it feels like you're pushing me away."

Mel winced, understanding the depth of Lacy's frustration. "I'm sorry. I'm not the best at managing my emotions around you." She dropped her eyes.

Lacy refused to look away, her expression troubled. "I don't know what that means. Around me? Why?"

Mel fidgeted. "I just—my feelings for you aren't easy to...it's...look, can we just—deal with the work stuff first? I feel like I need to get it out of the way."

Lacy nodded. "Okay. I can try. It's hard for me when it feels like I'm being pulled back into work-related issues while we're still trying to figure out what's going on between us."

Mel's heart ached. "I didn't want it to feel that way. I was just trying to get the presentation done."

"I get that," Lacy said, her tone softening slightly. "But it's hard to separate the professional from the personal with you."

Mel nodded, her frustration evident. "I'm sorry for making things more complicated."

There was a moment of silence as Lacy took a deep breath. "So, what ended up happening with the presentation?"

Mel hesitated, then decided to be honest. "The client liked it. And they specifically requested that you work on the next project with me. It's a big opportunity, but it means you'll have to decide if you're willing to come back and work with me again."

Lacy's eyes widened. "I didn't know that."

Mel smiled with some mixture of pride and sorrow as she explained, "They were impressed with the work you did and your passion for it, and they want you on the team."

Lacy sat back, absorbing the news. "I see. Well, that's something to think about."

"Yeah. I get it if you need time to decide. I just didn't want to leave things unresolved."

Lacy looked at her, a mixture of emotions flickering in her eyes. "It's not just about the work, Mel. It's about what's happening between us."

Mel's heart ached as she heard this. "I know. I want this—I want us to try to be something more. If you're willing to give it a shot. You don't have to answer me right now, just... think about it? Please."

Lacy took a deep breath. "Okay. I'll think about it."

Mel nodded, feeling a mix of relief and disappointment. "That's all I can ask."

As Lacy prepared to leave, Mel felt a sudden surge of desperation. She needed to explain something she had kept hidden for far too long. "Lacy, before you go...there's something else I need to explain. It's about that time with Chet."

Lacy stiffened, apprehensive. "I don't know that I want to talk about that."

Mel took a deep breath, her mind racing. "Please, just. I need you to know the truth. Chet...I was just trying to figure out if I could like a guy. I was trying to prove that if I could like Chet, I could like guys. I've never been straight, not really. And—I had feelings for you that I wasn't comfortable with. Because of our situation...I was tutoring you, and you seemed so—this sounds awful, I know—innocent, I guess. Chet was just a way to test something I already knew deep down."

Lacy's eyes softened, but her expression remained guarded. "Okay."

Mel continued, her voice trembling. "When I got to college, I tried to experiment with women, but it was all... superficial. I didn't have real feelings for anyone. I was bad at relationships, and I didn't know what I wanted. I just need you to know that I had feelings for you then. I have feelings for you now. And—look, I know it's ridiculous, but I miss you. I miss us. Even if it's not perfect, I'd like to see if there's a chance."

Lacy looked at Mel, her gaze intense and conflicted. "Mel..."

Before Mel could say anything more, Lacy stepped forward and kissed her. The kiss was sudden, a wordless expression of the emotions they had both been holding back. Mel froze for an instant, and then she kissed Lacy back, feeling a surge of relief and longing.

When they finally pulled away, Lacy looked at Mel with a mixture of determination and vulnerability. "I don't want to leave things like this anymore. But we need to be honest with each other."

Mel nodded, her heart pounding. "I want us to be honest, too."

Lacy took a deep breath, her resolve clear. "Then let's figure this out together. But we have to take it one step at a time. And if I stay here, I'm not going to be able to hold myself back for very long."

"What if I don't want you to hold back?" Mel asked, unsure if she was ready for another rejection.

"I—" Lacy paused, staring at Mel, the intensity of her gaze making Mel hot all over. "I want to, Mel. I do. But just give me a little more time?"

Mel nodded, feeling a glimmer of hope despite the uncertainty. As Lacy gathered her things to leave, Mel watched her with a mixture of hope and trepidation. For the first time in a long time, Mel felt like she had a chance to make things right.

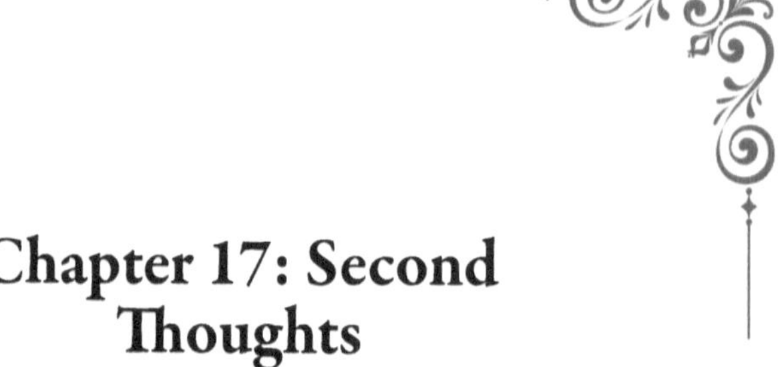

Chapter 17: Second Thoughts

The late summer evening sun cast a golden hue over the city as Mel and Lacy stepped out of a dimly lit restaurant, hands intertwined. The promise of a fresh start hung between them, palpable and hopeful. After their conversation the day before, they had decided to give their relationship a chance, to explore the possibility of something more. But as they walked side by side, Lacy couldn't shake a feeling of unease.

Their dinner had been pleasant—filled with easy conversation and shared laughter—but as they strolled along the bustling street, Lacy found herself replaying memories of the past, specifically those troubling moments with Chet and Bonnie. The idea of starting something new with Mel was overshadowed by the times her heart had been broken.

Mel seemed to sense the shift in Lacy's mood. She glanced at her with a hint of concern. "You okay? You've been quiet since we left the restaurant."

Lacy forced a smile, trying to mask her inner turmoil. "Yeah, I'm fine. Just thinking about... stuff."

"Stuff?" Mel asked, a teasing lilt in her voice. "You know, I'd love to hear about it if you're up for sharing."

Lacy hesitated, searching for the right words. "It's just... I've been doing a lot of thinking lately. About the past."

Mel's expression softened. "I get it. There's a lot there. But we're in this together, right?"

They continued walking, the rhythmic sound of their footsteps providing a semblance of normalcy. Mel led them to a quiet park nearby, a peaceful retreat from the city's hustle. They settled on a bench, and Lacy took a deep breath, trying to organize her thoughts.

"You know, I keep thinking about high school," Lacy began, her voice tinged with frustration. "I know you explained yourself, and I appreciate that. But then I keep thinking about how I felt after I saw you that day. I was hurt and confused."

Mel's face fell. "Lacy, I truly didn't mean to hurt you. I was trying to figure out who I was, and Chet was...a part of that. It wasn't about you."

"I know," Lacy said, shaking her head. "But it's hard to separate that from what's happening now. Every time we try to move forward, I find myself comparing it to the past."

Mel looked at Lacy, her eyes filled with empathy. "I want you to know that I'm not the same person I was back then. I've grown, and I'm still growing. But I'm out. I'll tell everyone at work. My parents. My friends. Whoever you want. I care about you, and I want to be with you."

Lacy nodded, her gaze drifting to the park's serene landscape. "I know you're trying, and I appreciate that. But it feels like we're jumping into something maybe faster than we should."

The silence that followed was heavy with unspoken thoughts. Mel's heart sank as she realized that their attempt to rekindle their connection was fraught with unresolved issues. She wanted to reassure Lacy, but she wasn't sure how.

"Maybe we need to slow down," Mel suggested gently. "Take some time to figure things out before we dive into a serious relationship? Just... date. Without commitment."

Lacy looked at Mel, her eyes reflecting her inner conflict. "That might be for the best."

Mel couldn't shake the feeling that they were standing on the edge of something, but she wasn't sure if it was a precipice or a new beginning.

As they walked to the subway, Mel reached out and gently squeezed Lacy's hand. "I'm here, Lacy. We'll figure this out together."

Lacy managed a small smile, her heart heavy with doubt. "Thanks, Mel. I appreciate that."

They said their goodbyes, and Mel watched as Lacy walked away, feeling a mix of hope and apprehension. The evening had not gone as smoothly as she had hoped, but she understood that their path forward would be anything but straightforward.

The following days were filled with a mix of awkward encounters and strained conversations. They tried to maintain their connection, but the tension was palpable. Lacy found herself second-guessing her feelings, and Mel struggled to navigate the shifting dynamics of their relationship.

One evening, Mel invited Lacy over for dinner, hoping to rebuild their connection. She prepared a meal with care, hoping that a relaxed setting might help them address their issues. As Lacy arrived, Mel greeted her with a warm smile and a hug.

"Hey," Mel said, her voice filled with genuine affection. "I'm glad you could make it."

Lacy returned the hug. "Thanks for having me. I've been thinking a lot about everything."

They sat down to eat, and Mel tried to make conversation. She talked about work, their mutual friends, and even tried to lighten the mood with some humor. But Lacy's responses were subdued, her mind preoccupied.

Mel noticed Lacy's detachment and felt a pang of frustration. "Lacy, if there's something bothering you, we should talk about it."

Lacy sighed, pushing her food around her plate. "I feel like I'm sending you mixed signals now, and I hate it."

Mel's heart sank. "I thought we were making progress. I thought we were trying to move forward."

"We are. I am. I just don't know if I know what the next step is."

Mel nodded, thoughtfully. "If you don't want things to get physical, I understand that. We can just... spend more time together. Get to know each other. The adult versions of us."

Lacy nodded. "Okay. That sounds...like maybe a good idea."

Lacy left, and Mel was left alone with her thoughts. The evening had not gone as planned, and Mel worried she was losing her grip on the fragile connection they had been trying to rebuild.

The next day, Lacy went for a run in the park, hoping that physical exertion might help clear her mind. As she ran, she couldn't escape the nagging feeling that something was amiss. She still wanted to be with Mel. But could she move past the heartbreak and embrace a truly intimate connection?

After her run, Lacy got a text from Art, who had come to town to see a play he was obsessed with. She met him for coffee, hoping that a conversation with a friend might provide some perspective. Art listened patiently as Lacy poured out her uncertainties.

"We're trying to figure things out, but every time we get close to resolving something, I end up feeling more confused."

Art nodded sympathetically. "It sounds like you're dealing with a lot of unresolved issues from the past. Maybe you need to address those more clearly?"

"I think you're right," Lacy said, her voice filled with resignation. "But I sort of feel like we have, and I don't know what else to do without making things worse."

Art offered a reassuring smile. "Just be honest with yourself and with her. She'll understand."

As they parted ways, Lacy felt a renewed sense of determination. She knew that she needed to confront her feelings, both for herself and for her relationship with Mel.

Later that week, Mel found herself sitting at her desk, feeling a mixture of frustration and hope. She had been working hard to balance her personal and professional life, but the strain was beginning to take its toll. She missed the connection and understanding that she had once shared with Lacy, and she was determined to find a way to rebuild their relationship.

Mel decided to send Lacy a message, hoping to make amends and offer an olive branch, but she wasn't sure how to approach the situation.

"Hey, Lacy. I know things have been rough lately, but I want to talk. Can we meet up and discuss things? I think we owe it to ourselves to try and figure this out."

Lacy's response came later that day, and Mel's heart skipped a beat as she read it. "I'm open to talking. How about the park near your place, tomorrow around 3?"

Mel felt a surge of hope as she read Lacy's message. She knew that their journey wasn't over, and that there was still a chance to find clarity and connection. She resolved to approach the meeting with an open heart and a willingness to listen.

The next afternoon, Mel arrived at the park, her heart pounding with anticipation. She spotted Lacy already sitting on a bench, gaze fixed on the horizon. Mel approached cautiously, feeling a mix of nervousness and determination.

"Hey," Mel said softly as she reached Lacy.

Lacy looked up, her expression guarded but hopeful. "Hi, Mel. Thanks for coming."

They sat together on the bench, the park's serene atmosphere providing a stark contrast to the turbulence of their emotions. Mel took a deep breath, trying to gather her thoughts.

"I've been doing a lot of thinking," Mel began. "About what we need to do to move forward."

Lacy nodded, her eyes reflecting her inner conflict. "I've been thinking a lot too. I need to address some of the feelings I've been holding onto."

Mel's heart ached as she listened. "I know things haven't been easy, and I'm sorry for the mixed signals."

Lacy looked at Mel, her gaze filled with vulnerability. "They're my fault, too. I just keep seeing you with Chet and Bonnie, and even when I try to move past it, I can't."

Mel nodded, her eyes filled with understanding. "I get it. And I'm here to support you. Whatever you need to do, I'm with you."

Lacy took a deep breath, her expression resolute. "What if we tried to spend more time together outside of work? I know we said we'd date casually, but I think I'd like to try more than that. To really get to know each other."

Mel smiled, hope finally blooming. "I'd like that," she admitted. Lacy smiled back.

As they left the park, Mel came up with another idea she hoped would move things forward for them both. Even though it would come at a cost.

Chapter 18: A New Perspective

Mel sat in Sophie's office, the air heavy with the weight of her decision. The room was quiet except for the faint hum of the air conditioning and the soft ticking of a clock on the wall. Sophie leaned back in her chair, her gaze steady and patient as she watched Mel fidgeting with her hands.

Mel spoke finally, her voice tinged with frustration. "My feelings for Lacy are complicating things. I care about her deeply, but I know if I keep working closely with her, it will affect my performance."

Sophie nodded, her expression understanding. "What exactly is making it so difficult for you? I thought being in different departments would help."

Mel took a deep breath, trying to organize her thoughts. "I just feel like being around her all the time and not being able to be with her in the way I want to makes me feel trapped. I want to make things work with Lacy, but I also need to be able to do my job well."

Sophie's eyes were thoughtful as she listened. "You're dealing with a lot right now. It's not just about how you feel about Lacy; it's about whether you can be effective in your role. Have you considered what the impact might be if you continue in this situation?"

Mel nodded slowly. "I've been thinking about moving to another organization. It seems like the only way I can get the distance I need to focus on my work without all the emotional baggage."

Sophie's expression was neutral but inquisitive. "Carver is a significant place in the ad world. It's a big step to leave. And we'd be at a loss without you. Do you really think moving is the best choice? What would you gain by moving?"

Mel sighed deeply. "I know it's a significant decision. Carver has been a huge stepping stone for me, and leaving it feels like giving up on something important. But at the same time, if I can't function effectively here, am I really doing Carver—or myself—any favors by staying?"

Sophie gave Mel a supportive nod. "You're right to consider both short-term and long-term implications. I can give you advice, but the decision has to be yours. It's about what you believe will allow you to be the best version of yourself."

Mel looked down at her hands, feeling a mix of anxiety and determination. "I need to think about what's best for me right now, and I don't want to make a hasty decision. But I just wanted to keep you in the loop about where I am."

Sophie smiled gently. "Take your time. We'll support you. Just make sure you're making the choice that feels right for you."

Lacy sat at her kitchen table, the late afternoon light casting long shadows across the room. Art was across from her, eating his dinner while Lacy pushed her food around her plate. Her frustration was palpable.

Lacy leaned back in her chair, her gaze distant. "I don't know if staying at Carver is the right choice anymore. I'm considering moving to a different organization. But I still have these feelings for Mel, and I don't know if I can just walk away from them."

Art's tone was thoughtful. "If staying there is causing you stress and making you unhappy, it might be worth considering a change. But do it for the right reasons, not just because you're frustrated. You seemed like you were loving it."

"Well...I don't want to make a rash decision. I need to figure out what's best for me and my future, I know that. But it's hard to separate my feelings for Mel from my professional choices."

Art nodded. "There's no easy answer. Just remember that your happiness and well-being should be your top priority. Whatever decision you make, make sure it's something that will benefit you. Put Lacy first for once."

The next day at work, Lacy was in the conference room, going over the project she'd been working on with Mel. As she looked up, she saw Mel walking down the hallway, heading straight for Sophie's office. Lacy's heart sank, and she couldn't help but worry about what that might mean.

Mel didn't glance in Lacy's direction as she passed by. Lacy's anxiety grew as she wondered what decision Mel might have made and how it would affect their future.

Lacy's phone buzzed with a new message, but her mind was still focused on Mel. She was anxious about the potential changes and unsure about what the future might hold for her.

When Mel finally emerged from Sophie's office, her face was set in a determined expression. Lacy watched her from a distance, trying to gauge the outcome of the conversation – but Mel wasn't giving away anything at all.

Chapter 19: Revisions and Rewrites

Lacy sat back at her desk, her focus fractured, unable to shake the growing tension she felt after hearing the news. Mel had resigned from her position, effective immediately. The message had come through HR—Darcy had even stopped by to make sure Lacy would be okay handling the upcoming project for a little while, since they would have to find a replacement for Mel—and Lacy had been stunned. The suddenness of Mel's departure felt like a slap in the face. How could Mel leave without a word? Had she really decided that their relationship wasn't worth the effort?

The afternoon dragged on, each minute feeling like an hour. Lacy's frustration simmered, and she couldn't concentrate on her work. She found herself staring blankly at her screen, her mind racing through the implications of Mel's departure. The thought of Mel leaving Carver, leaving her, made Lacy's heart pound with both anger and sadness. *She didn't even talk to me first.*

As the clock ticked closer to the end of the day, Lacy made up her mind. She was determined to confront Mel, to demand answers. She needed to know why Mel had left without even a goodbye.

Before anyone else left at the end of the day, Lacy was already packing up and heading out. Just as the clock hit 5, she was out the door. Lacy never considered herself a clock-watcher, but she had an important mission tonight, and she wasn't about to just let things go.

The building Mel lived in was just a few blocks away. As Lacy arrived, she stood outside the entrance, her breath visible in the crisp evening air. She called Mel's phone for the fifth time, but it went straight to voicemail. Frustrated, Lacy waited. She didn't know the apartment number by heart, and she wasn't about to start ringing buzzers at random. She paced back and forth in front of the building, feeling the cold wind biting her cheeks.

When it became clear that Mel wasn't coming home anytime soon, Lacy decided to take a walk, hoping to clear her head. The city was bustling with happy hour activity, and Lacy's thoughts swirled as she navigated the busy streets.

She wandered for a while, her anger slowly giving way to a deep sense of confusion. As she turned the corner toward her own place, she saw Mel standing on the sidewalk in front of her building. Lacy's heart raced as she approached, each step feeling heavier than the last.

"Mel," Lacy called out, her voice laced with a mix of relief and frustration.

Mel turned to face her, her eyes widening in surprise. She had been so lost in thought that she hadn't noticed Lacy approaching. *Very out of character*, Lacy worried. *Maybe something else is going on that I don't know about?*

"Lacy," Mel said softly, her voice tinged with an emotion Lacy couldn't quite place.

"What are you doing here?" Lacy asked, trying to keep her tone steady.

"I guess I'm just trying to figure things out, so I went for a walk, and ended up..." she motioned to the building, trailing off. Another unusual sign from someone usually so precise in her speech.

Lacy took a deep breath, trying to calm the emotions inside her. "Why didn't you say anything to me? You just left."

Mel cocked her head to the side, "Sounds familiar, huh?" then winced as she realized what she'd done. "I'm sorry—"

"No, no," said Lacy, backing away. "You're right. I deserved it. It's fine." She turned to go up the stairs to her building, but Mel followed.

"Wait. I'm sorry. That was shitty." Mel looked down at the ground, her shoulders slumping. "I just don't seem to know how to handle anything right now. I thought it would be better for you if I just left."

"That's not an explanation," Lacy said, her voice rising slightly. "You can't just make arbitrary decisions about how I feel about things."

Mel nodded, face etched with regret. "I know. I should have talked to you. I didn't mean to make things harder."

Lacy took a step closer, anger giving way to a deeper sadness. "I don't get it, Mel. I thought we were getting closer. More able to talk about this stuff. Why couldn't you trust me?"

Mel's eyes were filled with sorrow as she met Lacy's gaze. "I could come up with a thousand explanations, but I don't think any of them would make up for it. I'm sorry. Really."

There was a pause, the air thick with unspoken words. Lacy could see pain in Mel's eyes and knew that there was more there. She hesitated, then said, "It's cold. Come up for a little? We can talk about this...or not, if you'd rather just sit and watch some bad TV."

Mel hesitated, then nodded. "Okay."

As they made their way up to Lacy's place, the city lights flickered around them, casting long shadows on the sidewalk. Lacy opened the door and motioned for Mel to enter. The apartment was cozier than it had been. Art had helped Lacy string lights around the window frames, giving the place a more tranquil vibe than the white fluorescent that was for some unknown reason installed in the living room. *That's what I get for living in a converted warehouse, I guess*, Lacy had thought at the time. Now, she kind of liked that the space forced her to find ways to make it feel comfortable, rather than leave everything as it was.

They settled on Lacy's couch, which she tried to forget was also her bed, and failed. The weight of their earlier conversation hung between them. Lacy looked at Mel, her eyes searching.

"I've been thinking a lot about what happened," Mel began, her voice shaky. "I realized that I've been avoiding the real issues, which aren't whether or not I kissed Bonnie or Chet, but whether or not you could trust me to be with you and not just randomly end up with someone else."

Lacy nodded, her expression softening. "I get that you were trying to protect yourself, but it's not just about you. It's about us. If there even is an us."

Mel reached out and took Lacy's hand in hers, her touch gentle but firm. "There is. I mean, I want there to be. I've made mistakes. God, so many mistakes." She laughed, a hollow sound that made Lacy's stomach clench in dismay. "And I've hurt you. I'm sorry for not being honest at first about how I was feeling."

Lacy squeezed Mel's hand, her heart aching. "I wish you had trusted me more. We could have discussed everything at work, figured something out with Sophie—"

"No, not just then," said Mel. "I mean...ever. I had feelings for you for so long, Lace. All through senior year. I was in such denial." She reached out then, tentatively tucking a strand of loose hair behind Lacy's ear, her fingers lingering probably longer than they needed to.

"I don't know what to say to that," Lacy met Mel's gaze full-on.

Mel's face softened as she shifted closer on the couch. "I just...need to know if you're willing to give me a chance to make things right. For real this time."

Lacy's breath caught in her throat as Mel's touch lingered, fingertips steady on Lacy's cheek. She looked into Mel's eyes, seeing a depth of emotion that matched her own. "Do you really want that?"

Mel leaned in, their faces inches apart. "Yes."

Without breaking eye contact, Lacy leaned in and pressed her lips to Mel's, the kiss tentative at first, then deepening with a fervent intensity. Mel responded, her hands finding their way to Lacy's waist, pulling her closer. The kiss was filled with a mix of longing, relief, and desperate need.

Mel pulled away first, breath heavy, looking into Lacy's eyes. "I—can I touch you?" Mel asked.

Chapter 20: Breaking Down Walls

God yes, Lacy thought, then realizing she hadn't said it out loud, she gasped, "Please," and Mel kissed her again, this time with an intensity that left both women breathless.

Mel pulled Lacy to her feet, then lifted her, feeling Lacy's legs wrap around her waist, as Lacy kicked her shoes to the floor.

"It's so hot that you can pick me up," Lacy whispered into Mel's ear, and Mel laughed.

"Where's your bedroom?"

"Um...you're in it," said Lacy, and Mel looked around.

"Wait—what?"

"It's a studio, so...this is technically my bed," Lacy flushed as Mel sat back down on the couch, but she kept her legs straddling Mel, not wanting to break contact. "But the picking me up thing was still hot."

"It's a good thing these apartments are tiny, because more than a few feet and I might have some back problems."

"Aww, are you too old to have sex with me, because you can go if you want—" Lacy feigned getting up, and Mel grabbed her by the waist and pushed her down, this time straddling Lacy, guiding her back down onto the couch. Lacy looked up at her with an intensity of desire Mel had never seen before.

Lacy swallowed hard. She had wanted this—wanted Mel—in ways she'd never fully articulated. The smoldering look in Mel's eyes was more than she could have expected, and she wasn't sure she'd be able to survive if Mel didn't touch her—soon.

"Please," Lacy breathed again, her voice barely a whisper. Before she could second-guess herself, Mel surged forward, pressing their bodies together, the warmth of Mel's lips igniting a fire in Lacy's heart.

The kiss came like a storm—passionate and wild. Mel was insistent, coaxing Lacy to give in to the flood of emotion she had kept tightly contained. Lacy surrendered to the overwhelming need that consumed them both. As the kiss deepened, Mel's warmth enveloped Lacy, each moment igniting a spark that spread through her veins. It was more than just a kiss; it was a promise cloaked in heat and urgency.

"Lacy," Mel breathed against her lips, her husky voice sending shivers down Lacy's spine. "I want you." The admission hung between them, electrifying the air as their eyes locked in a moment of sheer vulnerability. Lacy felt her cheeks flush as Mel's hands slid down to her waist, fingers tracing a path that made her gasp softly. She was overwhelmed by the raw desire in Mel's eyes, a reflection of her own eagerness.

Mel captured Lacy's mouth again, this time more insistent, as if trying to consume every bit of the moment. Lacy's heart raced, excitement washing over her as Mel's hands began exploring her body, trailing lower with a sweet sense of discovery.

Mel pulled back just enough to look into Lacy's eyes. "Take off your shirt," she commanded, her voice rough with desire.

Lacy hesitated for only a second before obeying, fingers fumbling with buttons. Mel watched, her breath catching as Lacy pulled back the fabric to reveal her black bra. *Glad I wore a good one today*, Lacy caught herself thinking, before once again falling into the desire in Mel's eyes.

"God, Lace," Mel groaned, hands cupping Lacy's breasts through the fabric. "You're gorgeous."

Lacy whimpered, head falling back as Mel's thumbs brushed over her nipples. "Mel, please," she begged again, "I can't wait. I need more."

Mel's heart raced at the urgency in Lacy's voice. She unclasped her bra, letting the straps fall away from her shoulders. Lacy's breasts were bare, nipples erect. Mel swirled her tongue around one as she caressed the other breast with her hand. Lacy's body trembled with need. "Mel, don't stop—just—I need you—"

"What do you need, Lace?" Mel asked, her voice low. "Tell me what you need." She looked up, and Lacy's eyes locked onto Mel's.

"I need you inside me."

Mel unbuttoned Lacy's jeans—she'd been admiring how good Lacy looked in them earlier, but was even happier to be taking them off of her. She traced the edge of Lacy's panties, dipping beneath fabric to brush against the wetness between her legs. Lacy gasped, hips jerking forward. "Mel, please, please—"

Mel fought to control her own desire, but couldn't wait. She yanked Lacy's panties down, then touched Lacy, gasping at her wetness.

Slowly, she slid one finger inside, and Lacy cried out, "More, Mel, please—"

A second finger joined the first, Mel's thumb pressing against Lacy's clit. Lacy's cries grew louder, more desperate, as Mel moved against her. "I'm close—so close—"

Mel wasn't ready to let Lacy come just yet. She withdrew her fingers, watching as Lacy trembled with frustration. "Why did you stop?" Lacy asked, voice filled with need.

"Because I want to make you fall apart for me," Mel said.

Lacy's eyes widened with desire and surprise at this side of Mel—a side she hadn't seen before but was more than thrilled to find was very real and very hot and very—

Before Lacy could finish the thought, Mel's fingers plunged back inside her, this time with a third finger, pushing Lacy closer to the edge.

Lacy's cries grew louder, body shaking. Mel pressed her thumb harder against Lacy's clit, applying unrelenting pressure, till Lacy's body jerked as she cried out, her body convulsing as she came.

Mel watched, her breath coming in short, shallow gasps, as Lacy collapsed. Mel withdrew her fingers, licking them clean. She waited, enjoying the smooth serenity on Lacy's face, how beautiful she looked in that moment. But Mel couldn't wait for long.

"Lace," she murmured, her voice thick with desire. "I need you."

Lacy's eyes fluttered open. "Mel—yes. Anything."

"I need you to do everything you've always wanted to do to me."

Lacy paused. "That might take a long time."

Mel grinned, "Then you'd better get started."

"Close your eyes," Lacy commanded.

Mel obeyed. She could feel Lacy's breath on her skin, as she switched their positions, pushing Mel down onto the couch. She kissed Mel, her hands sliding down Mel's body, dipping beneath the hem of her shirt.

"Lace," Mel gasped, "Who knew you were such a tease?"

"You could have known a lot sooner," said Lacy, lips pressing to Mel's neck, teeth grazing her skin. "I want to taste you."

Mel pulled her clothes off, and Lacy smiled at the speed with which she got naked—then kissed Mel, a soft, lingering kiss.

"Don't make me beg," Mel said, voice trembling.

Lacy chuckled, making her way down Mel's body, leaving kisses in her wake. She tasted the sweat on Mel's skin, and it turned her on, and she wondered if it was possible for her to have another orgasm without even being touched. *I never have before, but that doesn't mean I can't now...*

She settled between Mel's legs and slowly started to lick her, grasping her hips as Mel bucked and cried out. Listening to Mel's body, Lacy found where Mel most wanted to be touched and settled there, making quick circles with her tongue till Mel cried out, shuddering against her, pulling Lacy's hair, which, Lacy realized, turned her on immensely. *That...is an interesting development*, Lacy managed to think, before she moved back up Mel's body to kiss her.

"Ready for more?" Mel asked, and Lacy laughed, realizing she was, indeed, ready for a lot more.

Hours later, Lacy blinked awake, her hand reaching out to an empty space beside her. Mel wasn't in bed, but the smell of fresh coffee infused the room. A moment later, Mel appeared, a steaming cup in hand, a soft smile on her face. She slipped under the covers, handing Lacy the cup, before pulling her close.

"Good morning," said Mel.

"It is," said Lacy, taking a sip of coffee. "Yep, I'm going to need that today."

"Oh?" said Mel, "Up late last night?"

"Yes, someone really kept me going," said Lacy, straight-faced. They both smirked at that, and settled back underneath Lacy's blanket.

Just as they nestled into each other, Lacy's alarm for work chimed, breaking the cozy silence.

"Damn," Lacy swore. "Work."

Mel's eyes clouded over. "About that—"

"No—" Lacy said, jumping up, "I'm going to be late. And I have to do extra work because of the client coming in this afternoon and you being gone and it's not your fault but I really have to—" And she was out of the room before Mel could even say a word.

While the shower ran, Mel checked her emails, and found the one that she'd gotten the night before about a new job opening. She smiled and wrote back.

Chapter 21: Second Impressions

Two months later.

The chaos of Mel's sudden departure had settled into something resembling normalcy. Mel had stayed true to her decision, stepping away from her original position.

But, to Lacy's surprise, she had moved into a different division at Carver, a strategic role that allowed her to flex her creativity while maintaining a distance from the day-to-day operations of Lacy's department. Lacy later learned that Sophie had offered Mel the job the same day she quit—so she really wasn't unemployed for long, and the two of them got to see each other in the office, even if Lacy was no longer Mel's assistant.

Lacy, for her part, had transitioned into a new role as Sophie's assistant, a step that offered her both a chance to grow professionally and, most importantly, a healthier distance from Mel's immediate workspace. *I'd be so distracted if she was nearby again*, Lacy thought, recalling the first few weeks of distraction when she had worked at Carver, unable to stop thinking about Mel.

On the surface, everything seemed as it should. Their professional lives continued in parallel, both dedicated to their careers and the work they loved. Yet, beneath that carefully maintained professionalism, there was a quiet intimacy, a connection that had evolved and deepened.

On this particular morning, Lacy was running late, and rushed into Sophie's office, only to find Mel already there. *Weird,* thought Lacy *She's not in this division anymore...?*

Sophie sat at her desk, glancing over some documents.

"Alright," Sophie said, handing over a few printouts. "Remember that client who specifically asked for you, Lacy?"

"Yeah, of course. Benjamin Porter," Lacy responded, the name immediately coming to her.

"He's coming back next week. And while I normally wouldn't do this, given the time constraints and the work you two did the first time around, I'll need you both on this project. Collaboratively. Can you handle that?"

Mel and Lacy didn't even have to glance at each other. Both nodded.

"Good. Mel, you'll be heading the pitch, of course. Lacy, I'll need you to make sure everything's prepared on the logistics end. Let's keep this smooth and seamless."

Mel nodded, focused on the details Sophie was laying out. "We'll need full specs on the campaign, right? And I'll get the creative over to Lacy by Thursday."

"Good." Sophie's voice was firm, but satisfied. "If you need anything, let me know. Otherwise, make it happen."

They both nodded, rising to leave as Sophie's phone rang. Without another word, Mel and Lacy headed for the door, their shoulders brushing lightly as they walked side by side.

As Mel and Lacy separated to go to their respective desks, Mel couldn't help but glance back, her expression unreadable for anyone else but Lacy. It was still surreal sometimes, even now, walking past each other like colleagues, when so much had changed between them. They had both taken a risk—emotionally and professionally—but they'd found their way.

Before heading off to her own desk, Mel paused at Lacy's cubicle, situated just outside of Sophie's office. Lacy was typing up notes from the meeting, but she sensed Mel's presence and looked up just in time for Mel to lean in slightly and whisper, "We're still on for tonight?"

The words were simple, casual even, but Lacy still felt herself warm from hearing a hint of desire beneath the question. Lacy nodded, eyes bright. "Of course. I wouldn't miss it."

Mel's fingers lightly brushed Lacy's hand where it rested on the desk, a brief, almost imperceptible gesture, but enough to send a spark between them. There was something reassuring in that touch, an unspoken reminder that, despite everything, they were stronger now, and more certain.

"See you then," Mel murmured, continuing down the hall, blending into the hum of office life.

The rest of the workday passed in a blur of emails and phone calls, but Lacy found herself glancing at the clock more often than usual, willing it to move faster, so she could touch Mel again.

As the office began to wind down for the day, Lacy packed up her things, trying not to seem like she was in a rush. She sent a quick message to Mel: *See you in 10?*

Mel replied almost instantly: *Can't wait.*

Lacy stepped outside. It was one of those perfect city nights—cool enough to feel refreshing, but warm enough to enjoy a calm walk. She made her way to the familiar spot where she and Mel were meeting. The restaurant was tucked away on a side street, and served some of the best chicken fried rice in the city.

When she arrived, Mel was already at the entrance. Her face lit up when she saw Lacy approaching, and for a moment, everything else fell away.

"You're here," Mel said, her voice low, as if it was still a surprise they'd made it to this point.

"I am," Lacy replied. "Ready?"

"Always," Mel said, and with that, she took Lacy's hand, pulling her gently into the restaurant.

Dinner was a stark contrast to the tension of those earlier months, when every interaction had felt fraught with unresolved emotions. Now, things felt lighter, more comfortable. Mel paid for them, arguing that she made more money than Lacy, and besides, Lacy had paid when they went to the movies last week.

After dinner, they strolled through the quiet streets, holding hands. Lacy felt a calm settle over her. They stopped at a park bench near the edge of the city, where the lights twinkled like stars. The sound of distant traffic and soft rustle of the trees filled the air as they sat down.

"I still can't believe we're here," Mel said after a long pause, voice thoughtful. "A couple of months ago, I worried I'd never see you again."

Lacy watched Mel closely. "I know. It feels... different now. Better."

"Yeah," Mel agreed, squeezing Lacy's hand. "Better."

There was a brief moment of silence, but it wasn't uncomfortable. It was just them, sitting in the quiet night, feeling the steady rhythm of the city. Mel turned to Lacy, her eyes filled with a tenderness that still took Lacy by surprise sometimes. She leaned in slowly. Lacy met Mel halfway, their lips brushing in a soft, familiar kiss.

When they pulled back, Lacy rested her head on Mel's shoulder, closing her eyes. The weight of everything they'd gone through—the ups and downs, near-misses and almost-goodbyes—seemed to lift just a little more.

"So," Mel said after a while, her voice teasing. "What are you doing later tonight?"

Lacy laughed softly, shaking her head. "You're impossible."

"Maybe," Mel conceded, a grin tugging at her lips. "But you're still here."

Lacy smiled, pressing a kiss to Mel's shoulder. "Yeah. I am."

And for the first time in a long time, she felt like she was exactly where she was supposed to be.

Also by Rand Gilbert

Life Lessons
Life Lessons
School Days

Retreat
Retreat

Standalone
Learning to Swim
Love & Warwick
The Assistant's Heart
The Librarian's Assistant
Second Impressions

About the Author

Rand Gilbert (she/her) is a queer writer from the New England area. She primarily writes LGBTQ+ romances, including Life Lessons, Love & Warwick, Retreat, The Assistant's Heart, School Days, and Second Impressions.